LONDON'S LOST RIVERSCAPE

Chris Ellmers and Alex Werner

Introduction by Gavin Stamp

LONDON'S LOST RIVERSCAPE

A Photographic Panorama

VIKING

VIKING

Published by the Penguin Group
27 Wrights Lane, London W8 5TZ, England
Viking Penguin Inc., 40 West 23rd Street, New York,
New York 10010, USA
Penguin Books Australia Ltd, Ringwood, Victoria,
Australia
Penguin Books Canada Ltd, 2801 John Street, Markham,
Ontario, Canada L3R 1B4
Penguin Books (NZ) Ltd, 182–190 Wairau Road,
Auckland, 10, New Zealand

Penguin Books Ltd. Registered Offices: Harmondsworth,
Middlesex, England

First published by Viking 1988

This book was designed and produced by
A H Jolly (Editorial) Ltd,
Yelvertoft Manor, Northampton

Printed in Great Britain by
Jolly & Barber Ltd, Rugby, Warwickshire

British Library Cataloguing in Publication Data
Ellmers, Chris
  London's lost riverscape.
  1. London (England)—Description—
  1901–1950 2. Thames, River, Valley
  (England)—Description and travels
  I. Title II. Werner, Alex
  914.21 DA684
  ISBN 0–670–81263–3

Library of Congress Catalog Card No. 86–51237

CONTENTS

REFERENCES

Frank C Bowen *London Ship Types* The East Ham
Echo Limited, London 1938

Thomas Burke *Out and About, a Note-Book of
London in War-Time* George Allen & Unwin Limited,
London 1919

A G Linney *Peepshow of the Port of London*
Sampson Low, Marston & Company Limited, London
(*c.*1930)

A G Linney *Lure and Lore of London's River*
Sampson Low, Marston & Company Limited, London
(*c.*1932)

H J Massingham *London Scene*
Cobden-Sanderson, London 1933

J B Priestley *Angel Pavement* William Heinemann
Limited, London 1930

H M Tomlinson *London River* Cassell & Company
Limited, London 1921 (*revised edition 1951*)

Virginia Woolf Extracts from 'The Docks of London'
from *The London Scene* The Hogarth Press, London
1982 *By kind permission of the estate of Virginia Woolf
and the Hogarth Press*

ACKNOWLEDGEMENTS

The authors would like to express their
thanks to Bob Aspinall, David Challis,
Frances Collinson, John Edwards,
Barrington Gray and Max Hebditch, their
colleagues at the Museum of London,
whose support, combined with that of Alec
Jolly, has helped to make this publication
possible. They are also most grateful to
George Adams, Paul Calvocoressi, Bob
Carr, Frank Hasler, John Jupp, Charles
Kellerman, Ray Newton, Patricia
O'Driscoll, Alan Pearsall, Edward Sargent,
Tom Stothert, Malcolm Tucker and
Elizabeth Wood – all members of the
Docklands History Group – who have
provided a good deal of useful information.
An especial acknowledgement is due to
Robert Harvey, who has supplied much of
the material relating to shipping. Jackie
and Ian Alford, Bernard Hunt, Michael
Smith and John Edwards have helped with
information regarding Thames Tunnel
Mills and Meriton's Wharf. Chris Ellmers
would also like to thank his children –
Dominic, Gabrielle and Leo – who share
his love of the river and have helped to
provide him with the time to write his
section of this book. Any shortcomings in
the text, of course, are those of the authors.
A final credit is due to the Port of London
Authority, who had the foresight to build
up a major archive collection – of which
this photographic panorama forms a part –
and subsequently place it in the care of
the Museum of London.

A Photographic Panorama

The Royal Research ship, *Discovery II*, at the time of her visit to London, in 1929.
Photographed off the entrance to the St Katharine Docks, with Tower Bridge
dominating the background.

Discovery II was one of the many unusual visitors to the Pool of London. Built to replace
Captain Scott's wooden vessel (now in Dundee), she undertook six oceanographic and
survey voyages to the Southern Ocean between 1929 and 1951.

Introduction

1937, the year when the Port of London Authority despatched a now anonymous photographer to record the appearance of the banks of the Thames from London Bridge to Greenwich, was also the year of the Coronation. With visitors flocking to London for the crowning of King George VI, it was a time to celebrate the history, importance and character of the capital of the British Empire. London Transport published a guide to London for the occasion entitled *Imperial Pilgrimage*; its frontispiece was an aerial view of the Port of London, seen through clouds at 8,000 feet, captioned, 'First Port of the Empire'. The author of the Guide was Robert Byron, who described how 'Tower Bridge looks down on the Port of London, whose forty-five miles of quays engage one-third of the whole trade of the United Kingdom. The wealth represented by the contents of its warehouses at any one moment is stupendous. Yet many visitors to London, and many Londoners, too, are unaware that London has a port at all'.

Today it is all too obvious that London has no port at all. Although, in fact, London is still the greatest port in Britain, most activity is now concentrated way down river at Tilbury. The old Port of London – as recorded in the Port of London Authority's panoramic photographs – did not long survive the passing of the British Empire. The ships and the barges – the very essence of the character of London for centuries – have gone. The warehouses, where they survive, are either empty and derelict or have been converted into flats or offices. It is a very sad story, and one that, only now with the redevelopment of Docklands, may yet have a happier ending. Three years after the Coronation, it was the bomber pilots of the Luftwaffe who were looking down through the clouds at the Port of London and the East End and the Docks bore the brunt of their attacks. The nights of the Blitz were lit by the flames of burning warehouses.

But it was not the Second World War which finished off London as a port. Right through the 1950s lines of barges filled the Thames and Tower Bridge still regularly opened for big ships. But times were changing and the great bascules moved less and less. It was the inability of the older parts of the Port of London to change, to compete with the expanding container ports of the Continent and other ports in Britain, by encompassing new radical techniques in cargo handling, which drove commercial shipping out of the upper tidal reaches of the Thames and ended the long career of the First Port of the Empire. The closure of London's seven purpose-built enclosed dock systems began in 1967 and by 1981 had reached the great Royal Docks between Blackwall and North Woolwich. The riverside wharves went the same way.

Yet the buildings thrown up by trade lingered on, albeit empty and unloved. In my schooldays in the 1960s I delighted in wandering along the quiet alleys between the gaunt, brick warehouses which lined the South Bank of the Thames. It seemed to me extraordinary then that so much dereliction, yet with so much potential for restoration for different uses, could exist so close to the centres of business in the City. Some change was then occurring. I went to see the elegant and sublime warehouses of St Katharine's Dock before they went. If only I had had the enterprise to go and see London Dock – the greatest and most interesting of them all architecturally and historically – before its Georgian warehouses came down in the 1970s, virtually unnoticed and without much protest. The docks were always a secret world, open only to the Thames and shielded from the rest of London by high walls and guarded gates. But there is also that ignorance of Londoners about London which Robert Byron noted: a snobbish, ill-informed indifference to the great swathes of London east and south of the City which contributed so much to our prosperity. Thank goodness that someone in the PLA had the imagination to send out that photographer in 1937.

The change, when it came, was shockingly sudden. The London Docklands Development Corporation was set up in 1981 and within a decade the banks of the Thames below London Bridge have been transformed. Most of those Southwark warehouses have disappeared; new buildings, office buildings, are springing up; flats – both new and in converted warehouses, now line the river below Tower Bridge. The riverside today looks very different from that recorded by the PLA's photographer half a century ago. Admittedly, the change has not been so dramatic and as total as the mid-Victorian transformation of the Thames upstream from Blackfriars, when the granite of Sir Joseph Bazalgette's Embankment swept away wharves, warehouses, inns and private gardens. Many of the buildings photographed in 1937 are still standing today and the Thames-side architecture is still littoral in character, with buildings fronting the river and rising straight from the shore. But there are many open spaces between the buildings now; it is all much less dense. The riverside is no longer one of bustle and noise. The buildings can be seen because there are so few ships moored in front. London is no longer a port.

The riverside recorded in 1937 was densely urban and confused. It was not, on the whole, very beautiful by conventional standards. Most of the buildings were strictly utilitarian, dirty and unloved. Virginia Woolf, in her evocative essay on 'The Docks of London', wrote in the 1930s how, 'If we turn and go past the anchored ships towards London, we see surely the most dismal prospect in the world. The banks of the river are lined with dingy, decrepit-looking warehouses. They huddle on land that has become flat and slimy mud. . . . Behind the masts and funnels lies a sinister dwarf city of workmen's houses. In the foreground cranes and warehouses, scaffolding and gasometers line the banks with a skeleton architecture.' She was describing the Thames below Greenwich; the riverside photographed here was taller and denser: a continuous wall of commerce with warehouse after warehouse crammed together, festooned with cranes. There were about three hundred wharves and warehouses concentrated here out of some 1,700 in all, scattered between Brentford up stream and Gravesend way down river.

That dirty, industrial riverside may seem to have a consistent character, but there were variations. The warehouses varied in date as well as in size. Some – the earlier ones – have that simple Georgian dignity in brick which we can respect as the 'Functional Tradition' in architecture. The later, Victorian, warehouses are less coherent as designs but still – as they were not merely for show – have a dignity achieved through function and discipline, with vertical banks of windows contained together between brick piers and under arches. And grimy, industrial buildings can have beauty: Virginia Woolf saw that: '. . . the aptness of everything to its purpose, the forethought and readiness which have provided for every process, come, as if by the back door, to provide that element of beauty which nobody in the Docks has ever given half a second of thought to. The warehouse is perfectly fit to be a warehouse; the crane to be a crane. Hence beauty begins to steal in. The cranes dip and swing, and there is rhythm in their regularity. The warehouse walls are open wide to admit sacks and barrels; but through them one sees all the roofs of London, its masts and spires, and the unconscious, vigorous movements of men lifting and unloading. . . .'

Not that the wall of commerce and industry was entirely unbroken, for a few stately buildings intervened: the Custom House, the occasional pause of Georgian elegance, at Wapping and at the Royal Victoria Victualling Yard at Deptford, and, above all, the miraculous grandeur of Wren's Naval Hospital at Greenwich, as palatial as it is unexpected on the curve of the Thames around the Isle of Dogs. Then there are the occasional, delightful survivals from an earlier period: a row of cottages at Limehouse, or an old Thames-side inn, like the galleried Angel at Rotherhithe, where Whistler made his etchings of sailing ships on the river. There are other brief interludes: a handsome Edwardian police station or a block of flats erected by the London County Council and but one intrusion of dramatic modern architecture in the shape of Goodhart-Rendel's new headquarters for Hays Wharf just below London Bridge. Then there are the power stations and the strange circular or polygonal structures which mark the point where tunnels pass under the river, and even, surprisingly, the occasional tree. And then there are the ships, in all their wonderful variety. I know less about ships than I do about buildings, but it is clear that the photographer recorded a world afloat which has gone. The Thames is the poorer without that dense mixture of riverside architecture which so enhanced the buildings behind. While further behind, rising above the dark grey-brown wall of dirty brick, were the church steeples – the powerful strange shapes of Hawksmoor's Stepney churches, the sweet wedding cake of St Mary's Rotherhithe or the spires of the Victorians – acting as landmarks and reminding dockers and sailors that there was another London beyond the docks and the river.

Those steeples survive today but most of the buildings in the foreground have gone. It would be easier today to make a new photographic panorama of the Thames, for the PLA's photographer must have had a difficult job, penetrating busy warehouses or exploring down alleys to find suitable vantage points for his camera. We – whether historians, topographers or just plain Londoners – owe him a great debt. Just in time, he recorded the visible expression of a central, momentous aspect of London's and our nation's history: the appearance of the greatest port of the British Empire at the height of its wealth and power. The present appearance of the same stretch of river is also an expression of our present status and character. It is still changing. Whether – visually – it is really a change for the better I rather doubt.

Gavin Stamp

Selected Riverscapes from the Panorama

Upper Pool

Pages 6 to 17

The riverfront of the City of London has known many changes through the centuries. Today the landscape is dominated by the modern office block. In the 1930s, however, the scene was very different although Adelaide House, an office block next to London Bridge, had already been built. The Upper Pool was hedged in by large and often grimy warehouse buildings. Short sea steamers moored alongside the wharves, discharging and loading their cargo throughout the day. The river was alive with the coming and going of tugs, lighters and barges.

Today a number of the older buildings still dramatically enhance this stretch of the river, though no warehouses have survived. The Tower of London commands an important place in the history of London and of the country, standing isolated from the rapid development of the City. Behind it, to the west, the Port of London Authority headquarters building at Trinity Square remains an impressive sight from the river. It was planned in 1910 after the formation of the PLA, Sir Edwin Cooper being chosen as architect following a competition. The building remains a symbol of the power and confidence of the Port of London in the Edwardian period, though not completed till after the Great War. Lloyd George, when he opened the building in 1922, spoke of London as 'the greatest port in the world'. Near Tower Hill there were many wine cellars; H M Tomlinson described how 'about the west slopes' he found 'open trap-doors of ancient vaults, letting out fumes of wines'.

The Custom House and Billingsgate Market complement each other in their different architectural styles. They mark the area of London's old legal quays, once the heart of the Port of London. The small alleys and passages which separated the legal quays have all disappeared. Upper Thames Street

to the west of London Bridge still gives some idea of what this area must once have been like, with its narrow streets running down to the river. The legal quays were established in 1558 to control the discharging and loading of dutiable goods. They were all located to the east of London Bridge, as its navigation was becoming more and more precarious for barges and small craft. By the late eighteenth century, the landing of goods was still restricted to the legal quays and a few sufferance wharves. The quays were open spaces allowing for the cargo to be stacked up, examined and then weighed by the custom officials. Behind them lay large warehouses for the storage of cargo. When the docks came to be built, the operators and owners of these quays lost much of their business and were compensated by the government for this loss. The legal quays continued to operate profitably as wharves. Their proximity to the main markets of the City led them to specialise in the handling of fresh produce.

The St Katharine Docks, situated very close to the City, have become the best known and most visited of all London's docks. The fine warehouse buildings, now sadly gone, were once clearly visible from the Tower of London and from Tower Bridge. The docks occupied only a 23½ acre site. They were built between 1826 and 1828 on the site of the Royal Hospital and Collegiate Church of St Katharine by the Tower, founded in 1148 by Queen Matilda. Some 1,200 houses and tenements as well as the Hospital and Church were pulled down to make way for the construction of the dock. This was a densely populated area and over 11,000 inhabitants were displaced. Thomas Telford was the principal engineer during the building of the docks, helped by Thomas Rhodes, one of his most able assistants. The compact and awkward nature of the site resulted in Telford designing two docks linked by a basin, with just one entrance lock, though with three pairs of gates. Philip Hardwick, the architect of the dock, must have worked closely with Telford for many of the warehouses had deep foundations and two floors of vaults. The most memorable feature of the warehouses were their iron columns which rose sheer from the edge of the quay.

Wapping and Shadwell

Pages 18 to 31

In 1720 Strype described Wapping as being 'chiefly inhabited by Sea-faring Men, and tradesmen dealing in Commodities for the Supply of Shipping and Shipmen'. In the eighteenth century, wharves, warehouses and houses, in an almost unbroken line, ran along Wapping Wall not unlike the panorama of the 1930s. There was a fashionable quarter to the north with squares as fine as any in London, where many successful shipowners and ship captains resided.

In 1801, when the building of the London Docks began at Wapping, a large population was displaced. This dock, known during its first few years as the Merchant's Dock, owed its conception largely to one man, namely William Vaughan. He was a London merchant who had actively campaigned for the building of docks in London. During the last decade of the eighteenth century he had circulated pamphlets promoting his ideas and those of his friends.

John Rennie, acknowledged by many of his contemporaries as the greatest living engineer, was the first engineer of the dock company. Today most of the London Docks system has been filled in, with houses being built on the former basins and quays. However, many of Rennie's original dock walls are now visible and they remain as a testament to the quality of early dock engineering and masonry. Daniel Alexander was the first principal architect and surveyor of the London Dock. His work was also of the very highest quality. Unfortunately, the five large warehouse 'stacks' once situated on the north quay of the Western Dock were demolished in the late 1970s to make way for Rupert Murdoch's News International Printing Works. These were arguably London's finest Georgian warehouse buildings. Apart from the Wapping Pierhead Houses, Alexander's work can be seen at

the 'Skin Floor', Tobacco Dock, where cast iron columns of a tree-like structure support a wooden roof.

Tomlinson evocatively described the feeling of walking down Wapping High Street. He wrote: 'The warehouses of that meandering chasm . . . are like weathered and unequal cliffs. It is hard to believe sunlight ever falls here'. The walkways or bridges which linked the riverside warehouses with those on the other side of the street contributed to the claustrophobic effect. He saw a man working high up at a loophole, 'at the topmost cave of a warehouse, which you can see has been exposed to commerce and the elements for ages'.

In the nineteenth century Wapping and Shadwell supported a large working class population, many of whom gained their livelihood from the docks, the river or riverside industries and wharves. In the 1930s Meredith & Drew, biscuit manufacturers situated in Shadwell, was one of the largest local employers. The housing conditions were of a very poor standard. From the early 1900s, a programme of slum clearance and building of council dwellings was undertaken by Stepney Borough Council and the London County Council. These included the Riverside Mansions Scheme, which overlooked New Gravel Lane and the River, The Wapping Estate, the St Katharine's Estate, and smaller developments such as Andrewes House in Old Gravel Lane. In 1937 major work was underway building blocks of flats at Pennington Street and at the Shadwell Garden Estate. These were not completed until the post-war period, when an even more energetic building programme took place. Today a similar hive of activity is underway converting the warehouses into luxury apartments, building new blocks of flats on cleared sites, the majority capitalising on the prospect of a river view.

Ratcliff and Limehouse

Pages 32 to 39

Two of the most famous riverside parishes, Limehouse and Ratcliff are wrapped up in an historical and fictional past. The lodging-houses and pubs of Ratcliff and the Highway were the principal haunt of 'Jack ashore'. In the eighteenth and nineteenth century it must have been a dangerous place to walk at night, with drunken sailors roaming the streets and robbers lurking in the dark alleys and passages. By the early twentieth century the area had taken on a seedy appearance. Thomas Burke described it as 'a dirty lane of poor lodging-houses, foul courts, waste tracts of land', and with 'mission halls exuding a stale air of diseased hospitality'.

To the north an ancient road led up from Ratcliff Cross Stairs, along Butchers Row and White Horse Street to St Dunstan's, Stepney. Close to the river, a network of streets met at the junction of Stepney East Station; Cable Street joined the Commercial Road and a road led off to the entrance of the Rotherhithe Tunnel, which opened in 1908. Rows of small houses lined the streets running off the Commercial Road. Narrow Street ran behind the riverside wharves, crossing over the Regent's Canal Dock. By this period the dock was owned by the Grand Union Canal Company. Large quantities of timber were discharged from steamers into canal barges and carried to the timber wharves which lined the Regent's Canal. In relation to its size, only eleven acres, this was one of the busiest docks in London.

Narrow Street proceeded on over the Limehouse Cut, which was built in the 1770s to link the Pool of London with the River Lea, passing the Limehouse Paperboard Mills, known as Hough's. This firm was a large employer in Limehouse, with imposing warehouses on either side of the street where women workers sorted the waste paper. Stepney Power Station was built by Stepney

Borough Council on the site of Blyth's Wharf. Coal was delivered by colliers and barges to the jetty. A large chimney, over 350 feet tall, was in the process of being built. This was to lessen the smoke and dust emanating from the station's lower chimneys, which blackened the surrounding area.

Apart from Dickens' description of Limehouse in *Our Mutual Friend*, later fictional writers, especially Sir Arthur Conan Doyle and Thomas Burke, used it as a setting for their stories. What attracted them was Limehouse's Chinatown. The Chinese community lived mostly in Pennyfields and along the Causeway, some even under the railway arches in Trinidad Street, and were known to operate gambling and opium dens. The bad reputation that Limehouse gained in the early twentieth century was based more on fiction than on fact. Writers were attracted, also, by the large numbers of sailors, of all nationalities, who stayed for a few nights or weeks before leaving on outbound ships.

Nearly opposite the Limehouse Town Hall, the Empire Memorial Hostel, built in memory of the merchant seamen who lost their lives in the first world war, provided sleeping accommodation for over three hundred sailors. In 1937, it was reputed that over 213,000 seamen stayed or used the facilities of the hostel, which included a cafe, a library, a concert hall and an employment bureau. There were numerous other hostels, some of high standing like the Marine Officers' Hostel at the junction of West India Dock Road and Commercial Road, others aimed at sailors and working men, such as dockers, who had nowhere to stay and could pick up a ticket from the East London Seamen's Mission in West India Dock Road for the Salvation Army's Hostel in Garford Street. There were also hostels of a less reputable nature. At this period, the Limehouse Fields Improvement Scheme was being built: one of the largest pre-war public housing developments in Docklands. By 1937, twelve out of the seventeen blocks of dwellings had been completed.

Millwall and the Isle of Dogs

Pages 40 to 55

'Many hours have I squandered on the ridiculous bridge of the Isle of Dogs, in sunlight or twilight, grey mist or velvet darkness, building my dreams about the boats as they dropped down-stream to the oceans of the world and their ports with honey-syllabled names – Swatow, Rangoon, Manila, Mozambique, Amoy–'
Thomas Burke in *Back to Dockland*

Until the early nineteenth century, only a few people lived on the Isle of Dogs. It is not clear from where the peninsula's name was derived, though one theory suggests that it came from the fact that the royal kennels of the Palace at Greenwich were housed at the bottom of the 'Island'. The Isle of Dogs was low lying and very prone to flooding. A lake had formed at the northern end known as Poplar Gut. The marshy fields, however, made fine pasture for large herds of cattle and sheep. Live-stock was often fattened here, before being driven on to Smithfield Market. Seven windmills stood along the western side of the peninsula, hence the name Millwall. These seem to have been corn mills and not drainage mills as has been written elsewhere. They were well known landmarks to seamen sailing up and down the Thames.

The West India Dock and the City Canal which had opened in 1802 and 1805 turned the Isle of Dogs into even more of an island. With the coming of the Docks the industrial development of the area slowly gathered momentum. Manufactories began to appear along Millwall. The Canal Iron Works, Sir Charles Price's oil crushing mill and Brown & Lenox's chain and anchor works were three of the earliest. By the 1850s the area had become one of London's heavy industrial centres.

The beginnings of shipbuilding and ship related industries on the Isle of Dogs stretch back to the eighteenth century. The early yards and rope-walks tended to be to the north, and were probably little more than extensions of Limehouse and Blackwall. With the advent of iron-shipbuilding, a number of yards were built by Scotsmen, who brought with them many Scottish shipwrights. St Paul's, a former Presbyterian chapel built in 1856 and known as the Scotch Church, still stands in West Ferry Road, though now used as a storage depot. The 1850s and 1860s marked the peak of the Isle of Dogs as a shipbuilding centre, though ship repairing remained an important trade up until the 1960s.

The Millwall Dock specialised in the handling of grain and flour, as well as timber. The grain and corn porters who loaded and unloaded the loose grain and worked the suction shoots of the grain elevators were known as 'toe-rags', because of the sacking which they tied over their boots and the bottom of their trousers.

In the 1930s heavy industry was still a major employer, though some of the old manufacturing sites had become storage and distribution depots. Maconochie Bros, the provision manufacturers, famous for their tinned foods and soups, had a major works on the West Ferry Road and employed many local men and women. This was a close-knit community on the Isle of Dogs, seemingly cut off from the outside world, though during the depression of the late 1920s and early 1930s many workers were laid off. The landscape was described by Burke as 'a flat stretch of dreary warehouses and factories, ... approached ... by a long curving street of poor cottages and "general" shops'. However, he spoke of there being 'good company, and plenty of it', with pubs and bars filled with 'sweaty engineers and grimy stokers ... men who have circled the seven seas'. Devastated by intensive bombing during the second world war, the industrial framework of Millwall never completely recovered. Many of those caught up with the war did not return.

6

London Bridge

In 1831 a new bridge designed by John Rennie replaced the famous medieval London Bridge, which had once contained a chapel, shops and houses. The stones from the latter bridge were sold and incorporated into various buildings around London. Two of the bridge's alcoves were placed in Victoria Park, Hackney. At the spectacular opening of the new bridge, King William and Queen Adelaide arrived by state barge. This bridge was in turn finally dismantled in the early 1970s and relocated at Lake Havasu City, Arizona, USA.

Adelaide House

This fine building survived the Second World War. J B Priestley described it in one of his novels as 'a grim Assyrian bulk of stone'. It dates from 1925, architects Sir John Burnet and Tait. Below, London Bridge Wharf occupied the site of the waterworks of the old London Bridge. In the 1930s this wharf handled general cargo. The MV *Lutzen* (339 tons gross) lies alongside, possibly discharging frozen salmon from Labrador.

St Magnus the Martyr

The church also known as St Magnus ad Pontem, stands at the head of the site of the old London Bridge. It was burnt down in the Fire of London of 1666, and rebuilt by Sir Christopher Wren.

The Monument

Erected between 1671 and 1677 from the design of Sir Christopher Wren to commemorate the Great Fire of 1666. The fire had started close by in Pudding Lane. In the late nineteenth and early twentieth century, oranges, bananas and other exotic fruit were sold regularly at the large Fruit Sale Room in Monument Buildings.

Fresh Wharf and Cox & Hammond's Quay

In medieval times, Fresh Wharf was one of the principal wharves for the unloading of fish. It became a legal quay in 1559, as did Cox's, or Cock's Quay, and Hammond's Quay. In the 1930s, Fresh Wharf Limited occupied the whole of the river frontage from London Bridge to Cox & Hammond's Quay. Of the two berths, the larger of 455 feet in length could accommodate ships of 7,000 tons. This was a busy wharf with over 100 ships berthing a year and with storage facilities for 20,000 tons of produce. There were some 28 cranes,

the newest being the Stothert & Pitt electric crane to the east of London Bridge Wharf. The wharves handled mainly canned goods, green fruit and general cargoes. Major work was underway during the late 1930s constructing a quay in front of the wharves and extending the existing jetty at London Bridge Wharf. In the post-war period, the MV *Monte Ulia*, with a gross registered tonnage of 10,123, was probably the largest vessel to operate a regular service between this wharf and the Canaries.

Nicholson's and Botolph Wharves

Nicholson's Wharf was named after its owner in the nineteenth century. It replaced three earlier legal quays. St Botolph's Wharf (page 7) was made a legal quay in 1559. It seems to have been originally called Buttolph's Gate and Stow remarked that it was given and 'confirmed by William Conqueror to the Monkes of Westminster'. In the 1930s, these two wharves were occupied by Nicholson's Wharves Ltd, who handled dried and green fruit, canned goods and general Mediterranean produce. A pontoon extended into the river allowing large ships such as the *Leopardi* to use the wharf. In 1934, there were a number of disputes between Nicholson's and Fresh Wharf, involving ships extending in front of the others property.

SS *Leopardi*

Built by the Tyne and Iron Steam Ship Co in 1915, and owned by the Italian company, Tirrenia Soc Anon di Nav. In 1937 she made a number of voyages between Genoa and London. She was subsequently torpedoed and sunk in 1940 by the British submarine *Osiris* near Tolmetta.

Billingsgate

London's principal trading dock from early times until the eighteenth century. With arcaded quays to the east and west, and a market to the north, small ships, barges and lighters would have used it to unload cargo. In the nineteenth century this dock was filled in when the new fish market was built.

Billingsgate Fish Market

Between 1849 and 1853, the old market sheds were rebuilt to the designs of J R Bunning and further enlarged in 1874–75 by Sir Horace Jones. Fish was brought here, in the 1930s, each morning by ship as well as by rail and road. Fish porters, with their white coats, can be seen standing on the main gangway leading into the market. The market closed in 1982, the New Billingsgate being relocated on the north side of the Import Dock of the West India Dock. The circular tower formed part of the Coal Exchange in Lower Thames Street, sadly demolished in 1962. Also designed by Bunning, the galleries of the exchange had elaborate cast iron railings and the walls were decorated with coal mining and coal handling scenes.

Custom House

Built between 1814 and 1817 (on the site of a number of the old legal quays) to the designs of David Laing. The front of the Custom House, facing the river was rebuilt in 1827 by Robert Smirke due to subsidence. This was the fourth London Custom House to be erected, the former ones being destroyed by fire. On the first floor, in the impressive Long Room, the London Tonnage Dues and Light & Pilotage Dues were collected. In the King's Warehouse, in the basement, goods were stored which had been seized by the Customs. The small custom service's launches were moored at the floating pier known as HMS *Harpy*, in front of the Custom House. To the west Custom House Stairs marked the site of Smart's Key, which dated from the early sixteenth century.

Custom House and Wool Quays

The first medieval Custom House occupied part of this site. It was here that Geoffrey Chaucer worked as Controller of the Customs in the late fourteenth century. In the 1930s a Dutch firm, William H Muller & Company, operated from this wharf. With over 125,000 square feet of warehouse space and further facilities at St George's Wharf, Deptford and at Morocco Wharf, Wapping, they were the largest foreign based wharfingers at work on the Thames. Their steamers, known as the Batavier Line, made regular sailings between here and Rotterdam, carrying general cargo and passengers. *Batavier V*, the outermost steamer moored at the wharf, was under German control during the Second World War and was sunk by a British torpedo boat in 1941. The innermost steamer, the *Batavier II*, survived the war and continued to operate a cargo and passenger service to Rotterdam until the late 1950s.

Humphery & Grey Lighterage Company Ltd

In the foreground can be seen Humphery & Grey's moorings at Battle Bridge Barge Tiers, on the south side of the river. The lighterage company of Humphery & Grey was formed in 1912 by the amalgamation of the two separate businesses, both of which dated back to the mid-eighteenth century. The new company was part of the Hay's Wharf Group and provided the vital link of transporting cargoes, in lighters, from the lower docks to the group's riverside warehouses. With a modern tug and barge building and repair yard down river at Point Wharf, East Greenwich, the Humphery & Grey fleet totalled some 300 lighters — exceeding 40,000 tons capacity — and seven tugs. Their craft bore a distinctive white Maltese Cross. The company ceased operations in the early 1980s.

Brewer's, Chester and Galley Quays

Galley Quay was made a legal quay in 1559. Chester Quay was of a later date, deriving its name from its owner in the seventeenth century. Brewer's Quay was, possibly, named after a brewery located nearby. In the 1930s these quays were used by the General Steam Navigation Company's vessels. General cargo, tea and wine were stored in the range of warehouses alongside. In 1941 Brewer's Quay was completely destroyed in an air raid.

SS *Starling*

The SS *Starling* was built in 1930 by the Ailsa Shipbuilding Company Ltd at Troon for the General Steam Navigation Company Ltd. She made regular journeys from the Pool of London to Hamburg and Amsterdam during 1937 and was berthed regularly at Brewer's Quay during the month of May. The vessel was broken up by T W Ward at Barrow in 1960.

Tower Hill

Until the eighteenth century this area of open ground behind the Tower had been used for public executions. In more recent times many of the dock union meetings were held here, in front of the Port of London Authority's Head Office building in Trinity Square. In the recent 'News International' dispute sacked printers often met here on Saturday night before marching off to the new printing works at Wapping.

Tower Pier

In May 1929 Tower Pier was first brought into use, having replaced the Old Swan Pier just above London Bridge. This became the principal place of embarkation for trips down the river to the Estuary resorts. The two principal companies using this pier were the New Medway Steam Packet Company Ltd and the General Steam Navigation Co Ltd. The Pier was also the headquarters for the Port of London Authority's Harbour Master of the Upper Reaches.

The Tower of London and Tower Wharf

Built in 1078 for William the Conqueror, the White Tower, the original fortress, still dominates the buildings, walls and towers which surround it. Prisoners were locked up in later centuries in many of the other towers. Sir Walter Raleigh wrote his *History of the World* during his thirteen-year confinement in the Bloody Tower. Sir Thomas More and John Fisher were put in the Bell Tower until their execution. It was from here that a bell was rung at curfew to warn visitors that the gates were being shut for the night.

The Tower of London was for many centuries London's main armoury. In the Bowyer Tower, long-bows and later cross-bows were made. A large and busy wharf in front of the Tower was used to load and unload weapons and gunpowder. Prisoners were brought by boat to the Tower and entered through Traitor's Gate. Here, at the stairs, the Constable of the Tower took them into his custody. At the Lanthorn Tower, to the south-east of the White Tower, a light shone out at night to help approaching craft.

Tower Beach

In 1934 a children's bathing beach and tidal playground some fifty feet wide was constructed on the foreshore in front of the Tower of London. The original shingle beach was transformed by the laying down of 1,500 tons of sand. This gave great pleasure to thousands of East End children both before and after the war, who were free to play there at low tide.

Tower Bridge

In the 1930s the twin bascule-bridge was in constant use, often being lifted over fourteen times a day. During the construction and after the opening of the bridge in 1894, the towage firm of Gaselee & Son Ltd was permanently on hand with one of its steam tugs to assist any craft navigating the bridge.

Irongate Wharf

In 1846 Irongate Wharf was destroyed by fire. New warehouses were constructed by the St Katharine Dock Company, the architect being George Aitchison. This wharf was leased to the London, Leith, Edinburgh & Glasgow Steam Packet Company. By the end of the nineteenth century the General Steam Navigation Company had taken possession of the wharf. This company operated regular services to many of the principal European ports from here and the adjoining wharf. In the 1930s general cargo was sometimes transported in containers as can be seen by those stacked along the wharf. Four large electric luffing cranes stood on rails on the quay and on the roof of the transit shed. Behind the wharf the top two floors of 'A' warehouse of the St Katharine Docks can be seen.

SS *Woodcock*

Built in 1927 by the Greenock Dockyard Co
Ltd for the General Steam Navigation Co Ltd,
weekly sailings were made from this wharf
to Leith. The GSN Co's steam tug, the *Gull*,
lies alongside her next to a group of lighters.
She was used as a stand-by for the company's
pleasure steamers leaving Tower Pier. Sold
to Vokins in the 1950s, she operated as the
Voracious, and was finally sold abroad.

St Katharine Wharf

In 1829 the 170-foot steam packet wharf
was constructed by the St Katharine Dock
Company for the landing of passengers from
steam vessels. In 1849 the General Steam
Navigation Co first leased this wharf from
the dock company. By the twentieth century
the berth was 225 feet in length, catering
for the small steamers of the GSN Co. Four
hydraulic cranes of 30 cwt capacity were
worked from the warehouses. The substantial
storage space at these two wharves included
bonded facilities for wines and spirits.
Thirty-two full-time staff and over 300 casual
workers were employed each day by the
GSN Co.

St Katharine Dock Entrance

The entrance lock was 180 feet long and 45 feet wide. By the 1930s only the General Steam Navigation Co's steamers regularly used this dock. The extensive range of warehouses with 40 acres of floor space stored a wide variety of goods including wool, tea, indigo, shells and perfume. These cargoes were mainly shipped into the dock via barges and lighters. The warehouses surrounding the eastern basin were destroyed by an air raid in 1940, and those around the western basin were pulled down to make way for redevelopment in the 1970s and early 1980s. The dock closed in 1968. Only 'I' warehouse with the bell tower (1858–60), and the dockmaster's house (c.1830) to the east of the dock entrance, remain standing today. The entrance lock was reconstructed in 1957.

Harrison's Wharf

This small wharf had full sufferance privileges in the late eighteenth century. Some of the warehouse buildings, built in the early nineteenth century, were demolished in 1986. In the 1930s the firm of Page Son & East operated from here; tea and wine being discharged from lighters into the warehouse. There were four barge berths and hydraulic cranes capable of a maximum lift of 35 cwt.

Apollinaris Co Ltd

This company imported mineral waters, and from the late nineteenth century they rented 'H' warehouse from the dock company. They had further facilities at Apollinaris Wharf, near Cherry Garden Stairs, on the south side of the river.

South Devon Wharf

This wharf handled tea and wool. Two mobile 15-cwt cranes discharged cargo from lighters. W W Jacobs' father was a manager of the wharf and no doubt some of his son's later short stories were based on events which happened along this stretch of the river. In the background enclosed over-roof conveyors can be seen linking the wool warehouses of the London and St Katharine Docks. The building below was a former brewery warehouse which predated the building of the dock and was known as 'G' warehouse. In the late 1970s, a small section of it was moved some 30 yards north to its present site and now forms the fabric of the 'Dickens Inn'.

Carron and London and Continental Steam Wharf

These two wharves were owned by the Carron Company, which was founded in 1759 and had extensive ironworks in Scotland. A regular service operated between London, Grangemouth and Glasgow. The Carron Line steamers could be identified by the cannon ball carried on their main masts. The steamer at the wharf was probably the *Forth*. The ample warehouse space included facilities for the bottling of wines and spirits, and for the handling of tea and other general cargoes. Fresh fruit and vegetables were discharged here for Covent Garden. There were two berths, the longest of 300 feet with hydraulic cranes lining the jetty and quay, one with a maximum lifting capacity of six tons. These wharves were demolished in 1974.

Hermitage Entrance

There was a small tidal dock here before the London Dock Company bought and developed the area in the early nineteenth century. The Hermitage Entrance, the second of the entrances into the London Dock, opened in 1821 for small ships, barges and lighters. It connected with the twenty-acre enclosed dock known as the Western Dock. The entrance had closed by 1909 and impounding pumps were subsequently installed. W Badger Ltd had a small engineering workshop in the hydraulic pumping station (1856) next to the entrance.

Hermitage Steam Wharf

There were substantial storage facilities at this wharf, which was owned by the London & Edinburgh Shipping Company Ltd. The berth was 300 feet in length. In the 1930s this company operated a regular passenger and general cargo service to Leith every Tuesday, Thursday and Saturday. Three ships were involved with this service, the *Royal Archer* (2,266 tons), the *Royal Fusilier* (2,186 tons) and the *Royal Scot* (1,444 tons). This wharf was destroyed by bombing in the last war. The London & Edinburgh Shipping Co Ltd went into voluntary liquidation in 1964.

Black Eagle, Brewer's and Albion Wharf

In the early nineteenth century, these small wharves with low level warehouses lined this stretch of the river. Not large enough to accommodate the later coasting vessels, they continued to store miscellaneous goods transported by lighter from ships unloading cargo in the docks or at the more modern wharves. Black Eagle Wharf was used by Truman's for the loading and unloading of beer.

Hasties and St Helen's Wharf

These wharves were built on the site of a seventeenth-century dry dock, known as Bell Dock. In the 1930s Standard Wharves Ltd, wharfingers, operated from these small wharves handling mainly canned goods.

Wapping Pierhead Houses

These two terraces, facing each other across the lock, were built between 1811 and 1813, to the designs of Daniel Alexander, for senior officials of the London Dock Company.

Wapping Entrance

This was the original ship entrance into the London Docks, designed by the engineer John Rennie. In 1805 the lock was 40 feet wide and 170 feet long with a depth of 23 feet. By the 1930s the locks of the London Dock had become far too small for the ocean-going ships of the day. Only those ships engaged in the coasting and continental trades entered the docks. However, the London Docks became a vast storehouse for a multitude of different cargoes. Wool, stored in many of the warehouses, occupied nearly a million square feet of space. Other goods accommodated included rubber, drugs, spices, ivory and coffee. In the early 1960s the Wapping Entrance lock was filled in and by 1969 the whole London Docks system had closed.

Wapping Old Stairs & 'The Town of Ramsgate'

It is reputed that the infamous 'hanging' Judge Jeffries was caught at Wapping Old Stairs while trying to flee to France after the abdication of James II. It seems more likely that he was caught at New Wapping Stairs as he was taken to the 'Red Cow', a public house nearby in Anchor and Hope Alley. 'The Town of Ramsgate', a small riverside tavern, was named after small packets and fishing boats from Ramsgate which used to moor near Wapping Old Stairs.

Oliver's Wharf

Built in 1870 for George Oliver in the gothic style, this wharf handled general cargo but had special facilities for tea. In the 1930s it was occupied by P R Buchanan & Co, wharfingers, who had a further wharf in Limehouse. Oliver's Wharf was one of the first of the dockland warehouses to be converted into luxury apartments.

Orient Wharf

This wharf had bonded warehouses where tea was stored and sorted into different grades. An overhead conveyor linked the wharf to warehouses across Wapping High Street. The leaden steeple of St John's Wapping can be seen above the warehouse roofs. Only the brick clock tower and the steeple survived the last war; the church was not rebuilt.

St John's Upper Wharf

Built in 1873, this wharf was commonly known as 'Jack's Hole'. St Thomas's Hospital owned the property. Barges and lighters used it to discharge and load general goods. Mud 'sweepers' appear to be at work clearing the barge bed.

Morocco and Eagle Sufferance Wharf

In 1936 the wharf was occupied by Wm H Muller & Co Ltd. It specialised in the handling of green and dried fruit, as well as general cargo. With its jetty there was a ship's berth some 210 feet long, with three electric cranes with lifting capacity of $1\frac{1}{2}$ tons. An overhead conveyor linked the wharf warehouses with those on the north side of Wapping High Street.

Eagle Wharf and Baltic Wharf

The two small wharves were occupied by Taylor Bros Wharfage Co and handled general cargo. Both wharves were under 80 feet in length, allowing only barges or lighters to tie up alongside. Baltic Wharf was destroyed by bombing in the last war.

Wapping New Stairs

These stairs led down to the foreshore. Access to many of the stairs was restricted in the 1930s, as children were found to be playing amongst the craft moored at the wharves. A group of children can be seen playing cricket in front of a lighter off Eagle Wharf, as well as a 'mudlark' bending down at the water's edge.

Old Aberdeen Wharf

Once called Sun Wharf, it was built in 1843–44 for the Aberdeen Steam Navigation Company. When the berth became too small for their steamers, they acquired and built a larger wharf at Limehouse. In the 1930s this wharf was occupied by the wharfingers, Taylor Bros. It suffered some damage by bombing in the last war.

Wapping Police Station

On the 2nd of July 1798, the Thames Marine Police Office opened at 259, Wapping New Stairs. The present Wapping Police Station, the headquarters of the Thames Division of the Metropolitan Police, designed by J D Butler and built 1907–10, now occupies this site. Next to the station, there was a small engine and boat repair facility for the river police's launches; some of these can be seen moored at the pier and on the foreshore.

Sun Hole

W H J Alexander & Co, who owned or leased most of this stretch of river frontage, used part of these wharves for the warehousing of supplies and for the maintenance of their tugs. From the small window built out from 'H' warehouse, Mr Alexander, the founder of the firm, used to watch over his tugs up until his death in 1929. St John's (K) wharf built in the 1840s is thought to have been designed by Sidney Smirke.

Steam Tug *Sun XV*

This tug was built by Earle's Co Ltd of Hull in 1925. A team of scrapers were at work on trestles. Their shifts would have been governed by the ebb and flow of the tide.

Tunnel Pier

The pier was named after the Thames Tunnel, located slightly further down the river. This tunnel was the first subaqueous tunnel in the world. It was designed by Sir Mark Isambard Brunel, using his patented tunnelling shield. His more famous son, Isambard Kingdom Brunel, worked as an assistant engineer on the project. The tunnel, begun in 1824, was finally completed in 1843.

Tunnel Pier marked the approximate site of Execution Dock, where pirates and smugglers were hung, their bodies tied to a post and not taken down until three tides had washed over them.

King Henry's Wharves

Used primarily for the storage of sugar and coffee, it was owned by W H J Alexander Ltd, but run by the firm of R G Hall & Co, wharfingers, who were also at St John's wharf. They had facilities for bonded storage, an open quay, and a heavy lift crane. In a contemporary advertisement they extolled their 'practical and expeditious handling of all classes of Free and Dutiable Goods'.

Thorpe's Wharf

In the 1930s this wharf was occupied by Cole and Carey Ltd, who handled principally canned goods and dried fruit. There were six cranes with a maximum capacity of 15 cwt.

Pelican Wharf

A number of small businesses operated from here in the late nineteenth century, including barge builders and a marble wharf. There was also a very ancient public house. By the mid 1930s the area had become a general ballast, sand and storage wharf operated by Nash & Miller. They had operated the barge yard but by this period had become wharfingers.

'The Prospect of Whitby'

This has long been one of the most famous pubs on the river, with its terrace looking across to the old entrance of the Surrey Canal. The pub was supposedly named after an eighteenth-century collier called the *Prospect* which was registered at Whitby and used to moor off Pelican Stairs. To the east of the pub stood an old barge building yard occupied by Allam & Son, though departed by this period.

Wapping Hydraulic Power Station

Constructed in 1893 by the London Hydraulic Power Company, it provided hydraulic power for the cranes and lifts of the private wharves along the Thames. The chimney and the accumulator tower can be seen with the roof of the engine house just to the right of the 'The Prospect of Whitby'. This station closed in 1977, being the last to supply power on a public supply system.

Dockmaster's Office

Built in 1831–32 for the dockmaster of the London Dock Company, it overlooked the first Shadwell Entrance lock.

Port of London Authority River Quay

The first Shadwell Entrance became uneconomical to keep open by the late nineteenth century, for the new Entrance Lock allowed far bigger ships and a larger number of lighters to enter the docks at any one time. In 1921, Sir William Arrol & Co Ltd, were commissioned by the PLA to fill in the old entrance and build a river quay in front of it. The work was completed by 1923, and cost nearly £25,000.

St Paul's with St James, Shadwell

The church was rebuilt in 1820, with only the crypt surviving from the 1656 building. Captain Cook was probably the most famous parishioner, his son being baptized in the church.

LONDON-BRUSSELS DIRECT STEAM
BRUSSELS SS. C? Lᵗ 28 BILLITER ST. E

King Edward VII Memorial Park

This public park was laid out in 1921–22 on land formerly occupied by the Shadwell Fish Market. There is a memorial, close to the Rotherhithe Tunnel ventilation and access shaft, to famous navigators, such as Sir Martin Frobisher, who set sail from Ratcliff on voyages to explore the Northern Seas. Behind the gardens, a line of pubs and houses can be seen running along what was once called Shadwell High Street leading into Ratcliff Highway, with the spire of St Mary's, Stepney on the skyline. This area was the centre of London's sailortown and such was its bad reputation in the nineteenth century that it was renamed the Highway.

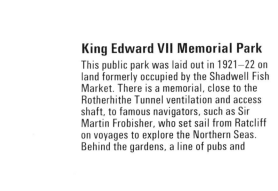

SS *Oranjepolder* and
SS *London Trader*

Oranjepolder was a Dutch-owned vessel which operated a weekly service to and from Rotterdam. The *London Trader*, a ship owned by the Free Trade Wharf Co Ltd, was built in 1934 by Hawthorn Leslie & Co Ltd, Newcastle and engined by Northern Eastern Marine Engineering Co Ltd of Sunderland. She made a regular weekly sailing to and from Hull, until torpedoed and sunk in 1940.

Free Trade Wharf

One of the busiest private wharves, commonly known as 'the madhouse'. The name Free Trade Wharf referred to the movement in the nineteenth century which supported amongst other things the repeal of duties on certain goods and of the Navigation Laws. This part of the river at Ratcliff in the eighteenth and nineteenth centuries was one of the principal areas for colliers to discharge their dirty cargo into lighters and barges. The westernmost range of warehouses was once known as Charrington's Coal Wharf. Most of these buildings date from the late nineteenth and early twentieth centuries. They replaced low level warehouses, yards and wharves. In the 1930s, the Tyne-Tees Steam Shipping Co Ltd controlled Free Trade Wharf. There were seven berths, the longest 400 feet in length, and over 20 cranes, one with a maximum lift of ten tons.

School

The school built in the late nineteenth century was originally called the Broad Street School. It was renamed after the war, Nicholas Gibson School, in memory of the man who founded the Cooper's School, formerly located nearby.

East India Company Warehouses

The first wharf to be known as Free Trade Wharf occupied premises formerly belonging to the East India Company. Two warehouses had been built in the 1790s, to Richard Jupp's designs, for the storage of saltpetre. In 1791 a major fire broke out at Ratcliff when a barge moored off the wharf caught light and the fire spread rapidly. It was reported to have been the worst fire London had experienced since the Great Fire of 1666. These warehouses were used by the Tyne-Tees Steam Shipping Company for the storage of general cargo. They were altered in the 1930s, concrete floors being added, although the original roof survived. They were the only two warehouses to survive demolition in 1985–86 of the whole riverfront from the King Edward VII Memorial Park to Ledrum's Wharf.

SS *Newminster*

She was built and engined in 1925 by Hawthorn Leslie & Co Ltd of Newcastle for the Tyne-Tees Shipping Company. She made weekly sailings to and from the Tyne. After the war, she was sold to an Indian firm and probably broken up in the late 1950s.

SS *Middlesboro*

Built in 1924 by Hawthorn Leslie & Co Ltd in Newcastle and engined by Shields Engineering Co Ltd of South Shields for the Tyne-Tees Shipping Co Ltd. Making weekly sailings to and from the Tees, she moored on chains at Stones Stairs Pier off Free Trade Wharf and discharged iron into lighters.

Beachcroft Buildings

These were London County Council flats, built just after the First World War. Much of the area behind Free Trade Wharf was rebuilt after the Second World War.

Ratcliff Cross

There were shipbuilding yards at Ratcliff at least from the time of King Edward III's reign. The name Ratcliff Cross recorded a cross which probably once stood at the top of Narrow Street. This and Ratcliff Cross Stairs represented for many sailors the point at which the Pool of London began and their voyages ended.

Phoenix Wharf

The wharf was divided into an upper and lower wharf. At the turn of the century, a sailmaker G T Crump occupied the top floors of the warehouse. Later it became a biscuit works. By the 1930s Luralda Ltd, tea-chest makers, operated from the Upper Wharf handling plywood. The church tower in the background was that of St James's, Ratcliff, bombed in the war and not rebuilt.

Trinity Ballast Wharf

From 1618 the Corporation of Trinity House had premises at Ratcliff. There was a toll payable for the privilege of taking on ballast, known as the ballastage. Ballast, usually gravel, was supplied to ships for the purpose of steadying them when unladen. The building probably dated from the late eighteenth century. In the 1930s, D T Miller had engineering and barge repairing facilities at the wharf. Behind the lighters at the Maritime Lighterage Co's anchorage buoy, known as 'Paddy's buoy', one can just make out, though blurred by the swell, a Gaselee & Son tug and a small oil tanker with her mast lowered.

Marriage's and Roneo Wharf

In the late nineteenth century this wharf was known as the Ratcliff Cross Flour Mill with the Globe Flour Mill alongside. Jacob Marriage was the owner of the former mill, hence the name of the wharf. By the late 1930s these two buildings were being used for the storage of general cargo.

London, Crown Mill and Black Eagle Wharf

These buildings reflected the once mixed use of the riverside frontage at Ratcliff. The mills overlooking the river would have been supplied with flour from lighters and barges. However, by the 1930s these had become general wharves operated by the firm of John Cooper, who handled mainly canned goods.

The 'Grapes' to Spark's Wharf

This stretch of river frontage was made up of early eighteenth century houses, which were being used by the middle of the next century as small wharves. The most westerly of this range of houses to survive, 'The Grapes', formerly the 'Bunch of Grapes', was the famous public house, whose interior was supposedly described by Dickens in *Our Mutual Friend* and called by him the 'Six Jolly Fellowship Porters'. Next door to it came Etheredge's Wharf, a small barge repairing yard also operating a business as lightermen. Then there was Barnett's Wharf,

a marine store, followed by Fielder's Wharf, another small barge repair yard. Lamb's Wharf, a mast and block maker's yard, backed onto Spark's Wharf. The firm of W N Sparks and Son built and repaired wooden sailing barges and lighters. This wharf was later taken over by Woodward Fisher, who were tug owners and lightermen. The original eighteenth-century roof trusses survive inside the building, where at one time barges were built. In the 1950s, Dan Farsons, the writer and television presenter, lived above the barge yard.

Duke Shore and Stairs

In 1660 Pepys visited this area on a num of occasions calling the place 'Dick Sh or 'Dike Shore'. In the middle of the eighteenth century a porcelain factory located here, though it proved to be sho lived. Duke Shore remained as a small where barges and lighters were laid up awaiting repair. This is one of the few of Docklands where the road comes clo the river.

35

St Anne's, Limehouse

One of the fifty churches built in or near London under the grant made to Queen Anne, the money raised by a duty on culm and coal brought into the Port of London. It was built between 1712 and 1724, the architect being Nicholas Hawksmoor. Inside the church, amongst the memorials, is a plaque to W Curling an eminent nineteenth-century shipbuilder and shipowner of Limehouse.

Taylor Walker's Barley Mow Brewery

In the eighteenth century there was a brewery as well as a distillery in Limehouse. The brewery was founded in 1730 by Messrs Salmon & Hare. The name of the firm underwent changes and by 1816, it was known as Taylor Walker & Co. In 1889, a new brewery was built on the site of the former Limehouse Workhouse. Later further extensions were made incorporating the old Limehouse Town Hall. It has been said that Duncan Dunbar, the famous shipowner who owned a wharf in Limekiln Creek, made his fortune from exporting Pale India Ale to India and Australia. In March 1941, incendiary bombs set the brewery on fire, halting brewing for nearly eighteen months.

Duke Shore Wharf

This was where Stepney Borough Council and later Tower Hamlets Borough Council tipped rubbish into barges. The rubbish was taken down the river to Queensborough to be used for land reclamation. A shipyard occupied this site in the seventeenth and eighteenth centuries.

Limekiln Wharf

From at least the late fourteenth century there were limekilns at Limehouse. Chalk was burnt to form quicklime, an important material used when making mortar for building purposes. Situated at the southern river end of Limekiln Dock, which was a natural inlet, the wharf stood on the site of an ancient shipbuilding yard. Dry docks survived here until the early twentieth century. In the 1930s R Passmore & Co Ltd used this wharf to discharge and load cement.

Dundee Wharf

In 1826 the Dundee, Perth & London Shipping Company Ltd was incorporated and by 1834 the firm owned two steamers, the *Dundee* and the *Perth*. From the turn of the century they had premises at Limehouse. In the First World War the shipping company lost three of their steamers due to enemy action. By the thirties, they were operating a twice weekly service between Leith and London. The names of their vessels, SS *Perth*, *London* and *Dundee*, followed on from those of their early steamers. The wharf occupied the site of a former shipbuilding yard. In the 1930s, its modern facilities included a large electric crane and over 100,000 square feet of storage space. The wharf was destroyed in the blitz.

MV *Arbroath*

Built in 1935 by the Caledonian Shipbuilding Co Ltd of Dundee, with diesel engines supplied by British Auxiliaries Ltd of Glasgow, for the Dundee, Perth & London Shipping Co Ltd. All her winches for the handling of cargo were electrically powered. She made a weekly voyage to and from Dundee carrying general cargo and passengers. Broken up in 1972.

Limehouse Pier

In the late nineteenth century this pier was run by the Thames Conservancy. Transferred to the London County Council, it was rebuilt in 1905 for their 'Penny Steamers', a river service which operated from Hammersmith to Greenwich. This proved very unprofitable and by 1907 had ceased. The *Primate* one of G J Palmer & Sons' tugs was tied up alongside the pier. The building directly behind the pier had been called the River Plate Wharf before becoming part of Dundee Wharf.

Buchanan's Wharf

P R Buchanan were public wharfingers who
specialised in the handling of tea.
Tea-chests would have been unloaded from
ships in Tilbury Docks and the Royal Docks
into lighters and brought up river to the
wharf. The six floor warehouse building had
over 100,000 square feet of storage space.
Mercantile General were one of the principal
lighterage firms supplying this wharf.
Buchanan had further premises at Wapping.
The major part of this wharf was blitzed.

Aberdeen Wharf

In the eighteenth and nineteenth century there was a shipbuilding and ship repairing yard on this site. In 1821 a company by the name of the Aberdeen and London New Shipping Company had begun to operate a service from Aberdeen to London. It employed a number of small sailing craft and, by 1828, steamers. In 1844, Napier on the Clyde built the Company a 1,100 tons cargo and passenger carrying steamer, called *The City of London*. The Aberdeen Steam Navigation Company had facilities at Limehouse by the mid 1870s. In the 1930s their passenger steamers, *Aberdonian* and *Lochnagar*, operated during the summer months, and for the rest of the year their cargo steamers, *Koolga* and *Harlow*, carried general cargo between London and Aberdeen. This wharf had special privileges for the unloading of canned salmon. The site was completely blitzed.

SS *Redcar*

Built in 1920 by Goole Shipbuilding and Repairing Co Ltd, and engined by Earls Co Ltd of Hull, she was owned first by the P&O and then by W A Wilson. In the 1930s, she made regular sailings up and down the east coast as well as making occasional voyages to the continent.

West India Dock

This dock system comprises three major docks, the Import, Export and the South Dock. Major works were underway in the 1920s and the 1930s to modernize the facilities and to make the docks more able to accommodate larger ships. A new entrance was constructed at the eastern end of the South West India Dock, eighty feet in depth and 550 feet long. Passages were cut between the Import and Export Docks, and between the South Dock and the Millwall Dock. In 1937, work had begun on Canary Wharf, located on the south side of the Import Dock. This was to be a new berth for the handling of fruit cargoes from the Canary Islands and Mediterranean Ports. Two of the Union Castle Line steamers can be seen unloading cargo overside into lighters using the ships' derricks.

Limehouse Lower Entrance

The original entrance lock of the City Canal opened in 1805, engineer William Jessop. In 1829 the West India Dock Company acquired it from the City of London. The canal became known as the South Dock or South West India Dock. It was enlarged between 1866 and 1870, the south side being widened and warehouses being built. This entrance had closed by the late nineteenth century. The impounding station was built in 1914–15 to maintain the level of the water in the dock. It remains in operation today.

Steam Tug *Culex*

This Gaselee & Son steam tug was built in 1924 by A Hall & Co Ltd of Aberdeen. Gaselee's had a tug mooring off Morton's wharf. The *Culex* was in the process of being repainted when this photograph was taken, explaining the lack of her name at the bow and the bands on the funnel being white and not a grey colour in the photograph. Gaselee's colour markings were a yellow funnel with three maroon bands. Gaselee and Sons had another very similar tug called the *Fossa*.

Morton's Sufferance Wharf

Morton's preserved and packaged all manner of foods. The business had been started in 1849 by J T Morton in Aberdeen. By the 1870s he had wharf and warehouse facilities at Millwall, occupying the site of an old oil works. This had formerly been owned by Sir Charles Price, whose seed crushing mills were one of the first major manufactories to be established on the Isle of Dogs after the building of the West India Docks and the City Canal. Morton soon expanded and acquired the Canal Iron Works site next to the Limehouse Lower Entrance Lock. Raw materials were discharged from lighters and barges into the wharves on either side of the tall factory building. The workmen of the factory formed a football team in 1885, which later became the Millwall Football Club. Morton's was one of the largest employers on the Isle of Dogs, their substantial premises extending across to the opposite side of West Ferry Road. They owned their own fleet of barges to ship exports from their factory to the docks. Their craft were amongst the last to be driven 'under oars'.

John Lenanton & Son Ltd

In the late nineteenth century John Lenanton acquired Batson's Wharf, just to the south of West India Dock pier. Timber was brought to the wharf to be cut using steam saw mills. By the 1930s the firm had grown considerably and occupied the river frontage south to Torrington Stairs. The site of the Regent Dry Dock formed part of their premises. Lenanton's handled all forms of timber including softwood, hardwood, plywood and wallboards.

'Torrington Arms' and Stairs

The public house was named after Viscount Torrington, the famous eighteenth-century admiral, and a member of the Byng family who had large land-holdings on the Isle of Dogs. The pub once stood opposite the stairs. Moored at the public buoy off the stairs was probably the tender *Ich Diene*, much obscured by the Thames barges, which was used by the Aberdeen Steam Navigation Company to ferry passengers from Westminster pier to their wharf at Limehouse.

Oak Wharf

Oak Wharf was formerly situated to the north of Torrington Arms Stairs. In the 1850s, John Fuller and Sons built and repaired barges at the yard near the stairs. To the south there was once a flour mill powered by steam engines.

St Luke's, Millwall

Built in the 1870s, the church received grants from the St Andrew's Waterside Mission for work among seamen. A mobile library, in the form of a hand cart, was taken around the docks. The church was bombed during the war and never rebuilt.

London and Stronghold Wharf

In the late 1930s, the two wharves were occupied by the Torrington Wharfage Company. Formerly, this site had been associated with the manufacture of wire rope. In the 1850s there were two wire rope manufactories alongside each other. Later in the nineteenth century, Bullivant & Co Ltd, the firm founded by William Munton Bullivant was based here. In the 1890s over 600 tons of wire rope and netting were produced each month. London Wharf was occupied at the turn of the century by the Foreign Bottle Manufacturing Co Ltd.

Millwall Central Granary

Grain was the most important cargo handled by the Millwall Dock. It was estimated in the 1900s that two fifths of all grain coming into the Port of London was delivered to the Millwall Dock. The Central Granary dominated this part of the Isle of Dogs. It opened in 1903 and was over 100 feet tall with thirteen floors. Four large pneumatic elevators sucked grain from the holds of ships moored alongside in the dock at the rate of over three hundred tons an hour. The capacity of the Granary was over 20,000 tons.

Millwall Barge Roads

There were important anchorages for barges and lighters, known as 'barge roads' down the western side of the Isle of Dogs. Two tugs, Gaselee's *Vespa* and a small Alexander tug are moored at the Thames Steam Tug and Lighterage Company buoys.

Hutchings Wharf

The wharf was named after Alexander and John Hutchings who, in the 1870s, had a manufactory on this site. They produced a patented wire rope as well as telegraphic and copper wire core.

Empire Works

Levy Bros & Knowles Ltd were manufacturers of sacks and bags. Formerly, in the late nineteenth century, the site included two lead works and the Salvation Army Wharf.

Millwall Dock Houses

Built in the 1870s for employees of the Millwall Dock Company. The easternmost range of these buildings survived until recently, when they came into the ownership of the London Dockland Development Corporation, who unfortunately had them demolished.

Millwall Dock Entrance

The only dock entrance of the Millwall Dock Company. The dock opened on the 4 March 1868, the lock being 450 feet long, 80 feet wide and 28 feet deep, to enable the largest steam vessels of the day to berth in the dock. The lock gates were termed 'box-gates', in that the riverside front of each gate was perforated allowing the water to flow in and out. The idea was that the gates would be better able to withstand damage when struck by a ship. The swing bridge for pedestrians can be seen swung back. In the distance, the roofs of A & B warehouses, built at the time of the opening of the dock, on the north quay of the outer dock, can be seen.

Workmen's Dwellings

The flats were just being completed when this photograph was taken. They were built on the site of Phoenix Wharf, where the paint works of Alexander Duckham & Company was once located. They were intended to provide accommodation for East Londoners under the Abatement of Overcrowding Acts. Containing over 150 flats in total, the different blocks, Montcalm, Montrose and Michigan House were named after the Canadian Pacific Steamers which used to berth in the Millwall Dock before the First World War.

Napier Yard and Millwall Ironworks & Shipbuilding Company

Two mid-nineteenth century shipyards flanked each other here on the south-west corner of the Isle of Dogs. In 1835 William Fairbairn set up one of the first major iron shipbuilding yards and, in 1837, David Napier established an adjoining yard for his sons John and Francis Napier. By the 1850s John Scott Russell had taken over Fairbairn's yard and leased part of Napier's yards, which had closed in 1852 during the construction of the SS *Great Eastern*. After the launch of the *Great Eastern*, the yard passed into the hands of C J Mare, and became known as the Millwall Ironworks & Shipbuilding Company. Joseph Westwood & Co were to occupy the Napier site from 1889. In the 1930s they were involved with the making of constructional steel work for buildings and bridges.

SS *Great Eastern*

In 1858 the *Great Eastern* was finally, after a number of attempts, launched sideways into the Thames. The largest and most spectacular ship ever to be built on the Thames, she was designed by Isambard Kingdom Brunel, with the help of John Scott Russell. While the ship was being built, vast numbers of people visited the shipyard to watch its construction and wonder at its colossal size. When the Westwood site was being cleared for redevelopment in 1984, some of the timbers and piles of the Great Eastern's slipways were uncovered. If one looks carefully at low tide, it is still possible to see parts of the timber slipway running out into the river.

Burrell's Wharf

In 1888 Burrell & Co set up a colour works on the central portion of what had been the Millwall Iron Works. Some of the old buildings, including the pattern shop and adjoining tower, existed at the time of the construction of the *Great Eastern.* Probably designed by W Cubitt, they were incorporated into the new manufactory. The sites on either side of Burrell's were occupied by metal works. By the 1930s the company had expanded on this site and was producing pigments and dyes for the paint industry, as well as varnishes and distempers. The adjoining Whittock Wharf was occupied at this period by the Free Trade Wharf Co.

St David's Wharf

In 1876 Perceval Moses Parsons took out a patent for 'improvements in metallic alloys', which involved the addition of 'ferro-manganese'. The Manganese, Bronze & Brass Co Ltd established a manufactory at St George's Wharf, Deptford. By 1906, they had acquired further premises at St David's Wharf. They were specialists in the manufacture of ships' propellers. Many of the Cunarders, including the *Mauretania*, had propellers made by this company.

The lead industry had long been established on the Isle of Dogs. In the 1850s Pontifex & Wood had once occupied the site adjoining St David's Wharf. By the 1930s it was known as the Millwall Lead Works, being an amalgamation of a number of different lead companies.

Owen Parry's Wharf

During the nineteenth century this area was occupied by a number of different undertakings. These included a steam washing laundry and a pottery. Owen Parry set up an oil seed crushing mill and later a varnish works. The site was finally used in the 1930s by H B Barnard & Sons Ltd, who reclaimed zinc and copper from scrap metals.

McDougall's Flour Mill

Another dramatic sight on the Isle of Dogs skyline until recently was the McDougall's Flour Mill. The original mill was constructed in 1869 on the south side of the Millwall Dock, standing alongside Hooper's Telegraph & India Rubber Works. It was rebuilt in 1902, and finally demolished in 1986/7.

Port of London Wharf

Directly to the west of the Port of London Wharf lay Ferry Street. A ferry had operated from here from at least the sixteenth century onwards, the site being marked by the 'Ferry House' public house. In the nineteenth century it was known as Potter's ferry and later as the Greenwich Steam-Ferry. The Corporation of London's Harbour Service had built the Port of London Wharf between 1851 and 1855 as their principal station, with a small dock in 1856–57 for the spare harbour service boats. The Thames Conservancy and later the Port of London Authority used this wharf as a storage depot for their equipment. The City of London coat of arms can be seen below the window ledges of the building fronting the river.

Felsted Wharf and Dock

In the 1920s Port of London Authority wreck-raising lighters were often moored in front of this wharf. It was let out by the PLA after they had ceased to use it as their river store. J Gregson & Co Ltd were ship joiners. On the wharf can be seen the dock gate, which would have been lifted into place by the steam crane. One of the PLA tenders was in the dock, probably undergoing repair. A wooden boat mould lies on the wharf to the left of the shed.

Millwall Boiler Works

This site began as a stone yard and then, in the late nineteenth century, John Fraser acquired the site and built a riverside wharf for their main boiler works, situated on the other side of Wharf Street. The Millwall Boiler Works had rolling machines for bending the metal plates into a cylindrical shape. Contained within the riverside building with the giant lettering advertising the firm, it is possible to make out the outlines of some of these machines. They included a large 1888 Smith, Beacock & Tannet of Leeds plate edge-planer with a bed of twenty feet. This would have been used to give the boiler plates a slanting edge, thus aiding the riveting, hammering and caulking together of the different plates of the boiler.

Livingston Wharf

This wharf was named after James Livingston who owned the Millwall Iron Works. By the late nineteenth century, the site had been taken over by The United Horse Shoe & Nail Co Ltd. They were to be succeeded by G J Palmer & Sons, wharfingers, motor haulage contractors, lightermen as well as tug owners, who used the site as an open wharf.

North Greenwich Railway Station

In 1926 the Millwall Extension Railway line closed. Over 60 years later the line was re-opened by the Docklands Light Railway. It runs through the dock taking a slightly different route, though re-using the remaining part of the Millwall Park viaduct. The new station at the bottom of the Isle of Dogs (Island Gardens) has been rebuilt further north. The original station came virtually right down to the riverside and it remained standing with its wooden canopy for many years after the line closed. There were four stations on the line, and in the nineteenth century the two terminal stations were operated by the Great Eastern Railway, South Dock by the East and West India Dock Company and Millwall by the Millwall Dock Company.

Calder's Wharf

In the 1890s a firm by the name of The Unsinkable Boat Company were located between the railway station and Island Gardens. In the 1930s this wharf was operated by J Calder & Co (1936) Ltd, wharfingers. The Poplar and Blackwall Rowing Club rented from Mr Calder a shed, which had once been part of the covered walkway leading between the station and the ferry, to store their sculls. The old station building itself was used as a changing room by the rowers.

The Greenwich & Isle of Dogs Foot Tunnel

The tunnel made the ferry almost obsolete when it opened. Built by the London County Council between 1899–1902, it was an immediate success. The passenger ferry rights were bought by the LCC on the construction of the tunnel. Thousands of people made the daily journey in both directions under the river to their place of work.

Island Gardens

These gardens, first known as 'The Island Garden', were laid out in 1895 by the London County Council. They supposedly owed their existence to Mr Will Crooks, the Member of Parliament for Poplar. The land, held by the Commissioners of Greenwich Hospital for many centuries, has never been developed for industrial use. The garden was known locally as 'Scrap Iron Park'. The view from the gardens has become justly famous, commanding one of the most perfect prospects in London.

Selected Riverscapes from the Panorama

Greenwich and Deptford

Pages 58 to 69

Of all the capital's riverside districts, Greenwich — with its rich history full of royal associations, and equally rich collection of fine buildings — has always been the best known to Londoners at large. In 1932 H J Massingham took a boat trip down to London's Dockland from Tower Pier and found, like many others before and after him, that 'Greenwich breathes serenity and reconcilement'. He was particularly struck by 'the sight of the Royal Naval College set like a jewel of unexampled lustre in that drab scenario between the Surrey Commercial Docks and the opening curves of Blackwall Reach'. The Royal Naval College, of course, had previously been Greenwich Hospital for retired seamen — immortalised in Antonio Canaletto's famous painting — and before that the site had been occupied by a series of royal palaces.

The nineteenth century had done much to create Massingham's 'drab scenario' of East Greenwich and Deptford, with a riverside of working wharves, shipbuilding and repair yards, ordnance factories, cable works, gasworks and electricity generating stations, besides London's first railway, opened — between London Bridge and Greenwich — in 1836. Despite all of this, Greenwich maintained its attraction for visiting Londoners, especially with the introduction of regular steamboat services in 1835. Even after the termination of passenger steamboat services in 1907, Greenwich continued to attract many thousands of visitors, mostly by the new pleasure launches. They came to enjoy the delights of the pier, the 'beach' on the foreshore, the Royal Naval College, the adjoining park and the Royal Observatory buildings.

During the 1930s Greenwich was London's best haven for shipwatchers. Frank Bowen,

doyen of London shipping, found it a good vantage point to observe:
'coasters and nearby Continental traders from the wharves and the upper dock systems, timbermen and big transatlantic traders from the Surrey Commercial and many others . . . Thousands of people stand on the bank there for hours but many more pay their penny toll to go on to the pier itself, a very long one, where several rows of seats are generally well-filled. For the comfort-lover the famous Ship Hotel of whitebait fame still offers a wonderful view from its windows.'

With the opening of the National Maritime Museum in 1937, the Royal Observatory from 1953–1967, and the arrival of the clipper ship *Cutty Sark* in 1954, Greenwich has added greatly to its unique mix of maritime attractions and is now one of London's most popular tourist centres.

Up river from Greenwich, Deptford presented a much more workaday appearance and A G Linney could write that Deptford Creek 'makes quite a little port of its own, with a flourishing trade in which colliers of some size and other sea-going steamers participate'. Deptford too had claim to a rich history, though here even the royal associations were of a distinctly working character — the Royal Naval Dockyard and the Royal Victualling Yard. Today important parts of these historic buildings still survive and Deptford is one of the few parts of the upper river where shipping can still be seen, at both Deptford Creek and Convoy's Wharf.

Rotherhithe

Pages 70 to 85

In many ways the great peninsula of Rotherhithe, stretching from the Greenland Dock to Cherry Garden Pier, had more in common with the Isle of Dogs than neighbouring Deptford and Bermondsey. Behind the busy riverfront — of working wharves, warehouses, barge yards and ship repair yards — lay the twelve docks and basins of the 300-acre Surrey Commercial Docks system. Between the two ran Rotherhithe Street, narrow and winding, strung out with a rich mixture of warehouses, ancient houses and newer council blocks, which provided homes for local workers.

Dock building began in the 1690s with the Howland Great Dock, designed as a refitting facility for East Indiamen. Sixty years later, however, the dock was much engaged in the northern whale fishery and its name changed to the Greenland Dock. It remained the only dock until the opening years of the nineteenth century when the construction of the Grand Surrey Canal, new docks and timber ponds, marked the beginning of a major transformation. By 1909, when the Surrey Dock Company handed its operation over to the PLA, there were fifteen interconnected docks, ponds and basins, besides the canal. Between the wars some rationalisation was carried out with the construction of Quebec Dock and modernisation of Lavender and Acorn Ponds. From the beginning, the Surrey Docks had concentrated on the handling of bulk cargoes of Baltic and North American timber and grain. With the opening of the extended Greenland Dock in 1904, however, cold stores were added for Canadian dairy produce and other foodstuffs.

Visitors in the 1930s were amazed by the peculiarities and atmosphere of this immense dock system: mighty Cunarders, in the Greenland Dock; and humble Baltic steam

tramps and sailing ships, in the timber docks; huge piles of timber on quaysides and vast rafts of timber in the ponds, which were also a haven for wildlife. These docks were, indeed, a secret place and even H M Tomlinson, the inveterate Dockland writer, found that 'exploring the Surrey Docks . . . will most likely present you, at the end of one quay of direct and unrelenting concrete, with the alternative of either a walk back, or a swim.' Small wonder that Mr Golspie, in J B Priestley's *Angel Pavement*, remarked that 'you never saw such a place. It's a hard day's work looking round the Surrey Commercial. Chap tried to show me once, but I gave it up.'

The Rotherhithe riverfront was also mostly given over to timber and grain — activities which had characterised the waterfront in the eighteenth century, together with a large concentration of shipbuilding yards. Rotherhithe Street, too, was an area of contrasts. Another famous river writer, A G Linney, had found ancient houses cheek by jowl with tenements swarming with children, and modern blocks of council flats. He also discovered 'sections of the way where no houses appear and a length of street is given over to trade, ricketty overhead bridges joining different parts of warehouses and mills.' Linney was fascinated by the mix of local inhabitants — 'typical riverside Londoners, quite a number of people of Scandinavian blood, dark-skinned southerners, negroes' — happily living together. So much was the area 'an island in the heart of London' that he came across many old folk living 'Down Town' — in the area of Rotherhithe's historic sailortown, around St Mary's Church — to whom 'the West End is actually as unknown as Timbuktoo'.

The destruction of the war years, the closure of the Surrey Docks (1970) and the river wharves, together with subsequent redevelopment, however, have all wrought major social changes. Rotherhithe now has fashionable riverside apartments and new houses built on the infilled parts of the Surrey Docks, mostly occupied by people from other areas of London.

South Bank

Bermondsey

Pages 86 to 95

The Bermondsey waterfront, seen in the panorama, was largely the product of mid to late nineteenth century redevelopment of earlier warehouses and mills. As densely built as the Rotherhithe riverfront, the Bermondsey warehouses were very reminiscent of Joseph Conrad's 'mad jumble of begrimed walls', of the 1890s. Dirty the warehouses may have been, but the photographs show many of them to have the walls around their loading doors coloured white by the continuous action of flour, grain, seeds and other bagged foodstuffs which were the main products handled on this stretch of the Thames.

Besides bagged foodstuffs, however, some of the larger warehouses – Chambers Wharf, Adlards Wharf and Butler's Wharf – handled an enormous variety of general cargoes. H M Tomlinson graphically captured the mood of Bermondsey's riverside on one of his visits here in the 1930s:

'Then we are lost in a maze of wharves and warehouses . . . Overhead was a criss-cross of bridges from numberless port-holes in old warehouses. Cargoes were trundling along the sidewalks, maize, syrup, salted hides, flour, and commodities for guessing at . . . Its storehouses and dumps have grown as would a forest from the waterside, the fecundity of industry without design. The walls of that complexity and huddle of brickwork were perforated everywhere, and apparently swarmed with burrowing men. From under the grimy crust of it, high up, the head of one appeared at an opening of its interminable galleries, and peered down'.

The physical remains of Tomlinson's Bermondsey warehouses can still be seen in Shad Thames, which runs eastwards from Tower Bridge around to the top end of St Saviour's Dock. A canyon-like street of tall warehouses, linked by overhead cast-iron cartways, Shad Thames is undoubtedly Docklands most evocative riverside street. Between the closure of the Butler's Wharf Company's warehouses (1972) and recent redevelopment, the atmosphere of Shad Thames captured the imagination of television and film producers and it was widely used for productions as diverse as *Dr Who, The Elephant Man,* and *The French Lieutenant's Woman.*

This part of Bermondsey, however, was no stranger to the attentions of the media. In 1838, Charles Dickens had used the squalid location of the pestilential Jacob's Island as the setting for the final chase of Bill Sikes, in *Oliver Twist.* Swept away by the sanitary reforms of the 1860s, Jacob's Island was the last of a number of small islands which had once existed in this low lying area of rambling watercourses, protected from the river by Bermondsey Wall. Indeed, Bermondsey itself is a derivation of an Anglo-Saxon place-name 'Beormund's Ey' – meaning Beormund's Isle.

Today, much of the Bermondsey waterfront is the subject of major transformation. Along Shad Thames, Conran Roche's massive Butler's Wharf scheme is underway to provide for fashionable shops, a hotel, museum, workshops and luxury apartments. Many of the warehouses around St Saviour's Dock have already been converted to apartments and in 1987 Vogan's Mill – the sole survivor of a once flourishing local riverside industry dating back to the medieval period – closed down for similar conversion. It is intriguing to think that some of London's most sought-after accommodation is only a hundred yards away from what had been one of the city's most notorious nineteenth-century slums.

Upper Pool of London

Pages 96 to 103

The building of Tower Bridge, which opened in 1894, and Tower Bridge Road cut boldly through the earlier Bermondsey waterfront, in typical Victorian style. In doing so, it created a whole new component of the river, whose busy activities were presented as a wonderful peepshow to viewers on both Tower Bridge and London Bridge. At high tide, the bascules of Tower Bridge were constantly opening – an average of fourteen times a day – to let large ships pass through to the upper wharves. Gaselee's tugs stood by to assist vessels in this and the wharves of the south side were the destination of a throng of short sea traders, coasters and lighters, carrying foodstuffs to the extensive warehouses of the Hay's Wharf group. This scene was evocatively described by J B Priestley, in 1930, in the opening to *Angel Pavement:*

'She came gliding along London's broadest street, and then halted, swaying gently. She was a steamship of some 3,500 tons, flying the flag of one of the new Baltic states. The Tower Bridge cleared itself of midgets and toy vehicles and raised its two arms, and then she passed underneath, accompanied by cheerfully impudent tugs, and after some manoeuvring and hooting and shouting, finally came to rest alongside Hay's Wharf . . . On the wharf, men in caps lent a hand with ropes and a gangway, contrived to spit ironically, as if they knew what all this fuss was worth, and then retired to group themselves in the background, like a shabby and faintly derisive chorus; and men in bowler hats arrived from nowhere, carrying dispatch cases, notebooks, bundles of papers, to exchange mysterious jokes with the ship's officers above; and two men in blue helmets, large and solid men, took their stand in the very middle of the scene and appeared to tell the ship with a glance or two, that she could stay where she was for the time being because nothing against her was known so far to the police. The ship, for her part, began to think about discharging her mixed cargo.'

By the 1930s, the Hay's Wharf group had come to own almost all of the wharves between London Bridge and Tower Bridge, storing there every variety of foodstuff – including three quarters of London's imported provisions – in what was popularly known as 'London's Larder'. It was an area, according to H M Tomlinson, where the smells 'were distinctly curious. A funny blended odour of the wood and straw of boxes of eggs, and of tea, cheese, butter and bacon'.

As one would expect, this section of waterfront – adjacent to London Bridge and the City – was the most historic on the south side of the river. During the medieval period the Abbey of Battle in Sussex, and the Priory of St Augustine's, Canterbury, had their town lodgings here. Another resident was Sir John Fastolf – who fought at Agincourt and was Governor of Normandy – later characterized by William Shakespeare. By the late sixteenth century, however, granaries, mills and brewhouses had made their appearance. A hundred years later, the wharves were also landing tallow, fats, skins and foodstuffs. During the eighteenth century, congestion in the port led to a number of the warehouses being designated as sufferance wharves.

In the late 1850s the proprietors of Hay's Wharf began a major rebuilding programme, the results of which can be seen in the panorama. The Tooley Street Fire of 1861 caused a temporary setback – it lasted a fortnight and was the capital's worst fire between the Fire of London (1666) and the Blitz (1940). Hay's Wharf was soon back to full activity after the war, employing over a thousand dockers, and it continued to operate until 1969. After its closure planning indecision created a long period of stand-still and redevelopment only began in the mid 1980s. The prestigious London Bridge City is now nearing completion with the conversion of the Hay's Dock and Chamberlain's Wharf warehouses to retail and office use, and the building of the new, private, London Bridge Hospital.

Greenwich Naval College

The Western Range of the King Charles Building of the Royal Naval College (North Western Wing), rebuilt in 1811–14 by John Yenn.

Greenwich had been a home of royalty since the mid-fifteenth century—the Palace of Pleasance, or Placentia, was situated on the waterfront and Henry VIII and his daughters, Elizabeth and Mary, were born there. King James I began the building of a fine house, to the south of Placentia, for his queen, Anne of Denmark, in 1619. The Queen's House was finished by Charles I, for his wife, in 1635. Charles II decided to replace the ancient and small Placentia with a grander Palace, started in 1663, to the designs of John Webb, a nephew and pupil of Inigo Jones. Building works were dogged by financial difficulties however, and William III and Mary converted the unfinished structure into a Hospital for superannuated sailors. With renewed fundings the talents of the nation's leading architects – including Sir Christopher Wren, Sir John Vanbrugh and Nicholas Hawksmoor – were brought in to complete the buildings.

In 1806 Nelson lay in state in the Hospital's Painted Hall. In 1869, due to a decline in the numbers of pensioners, the Hospital closed. It was converted in 1873 into the Royal Naval College, which still occupies the site. To the right can be seen the 1807 East Wing of the Royal Naval Asylum – part of the new buildings designed by Daniel Asher Alexander, architect to the London Dock Company – which later became part of the National Maritime Museum, opened in 1937.

Greenwich Beach

Immediately in front of the Naval College ran a riverwalk and, below it, a sloping beach, exposed at low tide. In Victorian times this beach was often crowded with visiting Londoners. Even in the 1930s A G Linney was able to describe it as 'quite one of the sights of the Port on the occasion of a summer Bank Holiday, covered with youngsters wading or bathing or sailing boats, and generally enjoying themselves at this little 'seaside resort', past which the traffic of London continues to make its way and give an added joy to the children'.

Further enjoyment was provided by Greenwich watermen, who would take passengers off the beach in their skiffs for a short row for a penny.

Greenwich Park

Stretching back from the Naval College, to Blackheath, is Greenwich Park, the oldest of London's Royal Parks. It was originally enclosed in 1433, and stocked with deer in 1515. James I walled the park around in 1619, and Charles II commissioned the layout of formal tree-lined walks in the 1660s, as well as the giant 'steps' which run down the hillside.

Opened to the public in the eighteenth century, the park also provided the home for Greenwich Fair, until it was suppressed for its rowdiness in the mid-nineteenth century. From the top of the escarpment the park still offers the best view of historic Greenwich and the river.

Greenwich Observatory

The foundation of the Royal Observatory at Greenwich in 1675 by Charles II, reflected the growth in scientific enquiry and the attempt to determine longitude accurately. The brick and stone turreted building, named after John Flamsteed, the Royal 'Observator', opened in 1676. The time ball, on the left hand turret was the world's first visual time signal – designed to be seen by shipping on the river – and has dropped at precisely 13.00 hours, since 1833. The 'onion-domed' building, on the left, is the Altazimuth Pavilion of 1899, which houses a 28-inch refracting telescope. The Observatory buildings stand on the Greenwich Meridian.

Greenwich Pier

The first passenger steamboat appeared on the Thames in 1815. By the 1850s the river was bustling with tall-funnelled paddle steamers, and a large floating 'steamboat-pier' had been built at Greenwich. In 1904 the London County Council took the pier over from the Greenwich Pier Company, improved it, and between 1905–1907 operated an ambitious, London-wide, passenger paddle-steamer service. Since that date the pier has become the focus of an increasingly busy pleasure boat trade.

Dreadnought Seamen's Hospital

Immediately behind Greenwich Pier can be seen the Dreadnought Seamen's Hospital in King William's Walk. From 1821 hospital facilities for sailors using the port had been provided in the hulks of warships afloat at Greenwich. In 1870 the Seamen's Hospital Society took the hospital ashore to the old Infirmary building of the Royal Hospital. This had been built to the designs of John Stuart, in 1763–64, but was much altered after a serious fire in 1811. It remained here, latterly as part of the National Health Service, until its closure in 1986.

Between the pier and hospital can be seen the granite obelisk to Lieutenant Bellot, of the French Navy, who died in 1853 looking for Sir John Franklin, the British explorer who disappeared in 1847 whilst trying to find the North-West passage.

The 'Ship Tavern'

During the nineteenth century the riverside attractions of Greenwich included a number of hotels famous for their whitebait and public dinners. Amongst these were the 'Ship Tavern', next to Greenwich Pier, the 'Crown and Sceptre', and the 'Trafalgar'. Whitebait, netted by local fishermen in their 'Peterboats', were cooked in batter and lemon juice and served within the hour.

In the 1930s A G Linney wrote of the 'Ship Tavern', that 'the bay window on the first floor is assuredly a spot which every American should spend an hour at during his visit to this country . . . Looking in either direction (always assuming that high water time is nigh) there is shipping on the move, and nowhere does one see more Thames barges tacking, criss-cross, from one side of the stream to the other'.

The 'Ship Tavern' was destroyed by enemy bombing in 1941, and the site is now occupied by the purpose-built dry dock which houses the famous clipper ship, the *Cutty Sark*.

Garden Stairs

During the 1930s it was still possible to hire working watermen to row passengers to riverside stairs and landing places in their skiffs, although few people apart from river workers still did so. River travel by watermen's wherries, however, had been popular until the widespread introduction of passenger paddle steamers in the 1830s.

Greenwich Foot Tunnel

The glass domed structure marks the southern end of the Greenwich Foot Tunnel, built by the London County Council between 1899–1902. Linked to Island Gardens on the Isle of Dogs, the tunnel – which is still in use – was popular with riverside workers as well as East Enders visiting Greenwich for a day out. This tunnel, together with Blackwall Tunnel (1897), led to the closure of the Greenwich Steam Ferry which operated a little to the west of here.

Dodd's Wharf

Greenwich Naval College, the Pier, the riverside walk and popular waterside taverns represented a welcome break in an otherwise busy working riverside. East and west of old Greenwich were power stations, gasworks, barge building yards, factories and working wharves. Dodd's Wharf – occupied by a marine engineering works and a ballast contractor – and the surrounding streets have now made way for an open space and a council housing estate.

Deptford Creek

Along Deptford Creek, the River Ravensbourne supported a variety of food mills, a gin distillery, engineering works, factories and wharves. Movable bridges over the river at Creek Road and on the railway line further south, allowed masted craft — as well as lighters — to navigate the three-quarters of a mile up to Deptford Bridge at high tide. A wooden bridge existed here in the fourteenth century built on the site of the 'Depeford', which gave its name to the area.

Although river activity has much declined, small ships and coasters still navigate the entrance to Deptford Creek, mainly with outward bound cargoes of scrap iron and steel.

SS *Falcon*

This London registered steam cargo ship was owned by the General Steam Navigation Company and is lying against their repair wharf. Built in 1927 at Troon, she was 214 feet long with a gross tonnage of 1,025. In 1937 she made trips between the company's Irongate Wharf and Leith, and their Brewer's Quay and Harlingen. This vessel was broken up in 1956.

SS *Royal Daffodil*

This twin screw pleasure steamer was owned by the New Medway Steam Packet Company. She had been built in 1906, at Newcastle, as a ferry for Wallasey. As a result of valiant service at Zeebrugge during the Great War, King George V commanded that the prefix *Royal* be added to the *Daffodil*'s name. The New Medway Company acquired the vessel in 1933 and operated it on their service between the Medway and Southend. In 1937 she briefly operated PLA dock cruises, before being sold for breaking in April 1938. She was unusual, for a vessel of this size, in having a hinged funnel.

The Stowage

The East India Company had begun fitting out merchant ships at Deptford in 1601 soon after receiving their Royal Charter. The enormous profits from these early trading voyages enabled the company to acquire land, to the east of the Royal Dockyard, to build their own shipyard in 1609. By 1614 the East India Company's interests in the area had grown to include: the shipyard; an ironworks for making anchor and chains; a powder mill; storehouses for timber, canvas and sails; a slaughterhouse and saltinghouse. The company storehouses, or 'storage', gave rise to the name of 'The Stowage', for both the riverfront, on the western side of Deptford Creek, and the street behind it.

Although the East India Company's interests in Deptford ceased in the 1780s, the area around The Stowage retained a strong interest in shipping. In 1820 Thomas Brocklebank had established a small shipyard in the Creek and built the paddle-steamer *Eagle*, which he ran between London and Margate. Brocklebank joined forces with other owners in 1824 to form the General Steam Navigation Company. By 1837 the company's fleet had grown to forty ships, carrying passengers and cargo to Hamburg, Rotterdam, Antwerp, Ostend, Boulogne, Dieppe and Le Havre, as well as the coastal ports and resorts.

To service and supply this fleet of ships, the General Steam Navigation Company had taken over Brocklebank's premises at The Stowage. By 1937 it was employing some 300-400 men in its smiths shops, plating shop, boiler shop, joiner's shop, sail loft and other stores. There were no facilities for dry docking however, and the work was restricted to fitting out, with the help of the two steam quayside cranes. Despite extensive bomb damage, the yard managed to work on some 300 small ships between 1935–45. It continued in operation until the early 1970s.

Payne's Paper Wharf

This interesting structure of six bays with semi-circular arched windows is decorated with stucco cornices and keystones. The three small electric cranes are busy unloading reels of paper from barges for the London printing industry. To the left of the building can be seen the western end of Borthwick Wharf. This massive building was a cold-store built in 1934 – to the design of Sir Edwin Cooper – for Thomas Borthwick and Sons, the meat company. Borthwick Wharf had storage facilities for 300,000 carcasses, brought here by insulated barges from the Royal Docks.

Payne's Paper Wharf building was originally the boiler shop of John Penn and Sons, whose main marine engine works at Greenwich were world famous. Engines were also fitted to a large number of ships here, including the armour-clad frigate, HMS *Warrior*, launched in 1860, by the Thames Ironworks and Shipbuilding Co, Bow Creek. In 1880 Penn's employed 500 men at Deptford and 1,200 at Greenwich. The firm amalgamated with the Thames Ironworks and Shipbuilding Company in 1899, and continued to produce engines and boilers until 1911, when the company ceased production.

In 1904 John Penn supplied engines and boilers for the ten paddle-steamers built by the Thames Ironworks, for the London County Council's 'Penny Steamer' service which operated between Hammersmith and

Greenwich Pier. Remarkably, the building seen here still remains, as does a cast-iron bollard with the inscription 'J Penn & Son Deptford'.

Behind Payne's Paper Wharf lay the site of Deptford Strond, the original headquarters of the Corporation of Trinity House from 1512. Trinity House had responsibility for the provision of both pilotage and navigation lights on the Thames and coasts of the

kingdom. It was also concerned with dredging the river and providing ballast for outward bound sailing ships. The Corporation moved to their new Trinity House, at Trinity Square, by the Tower of London, in 1787. A link with Deptford, however, was continued with members of the Corporation visiting their two hospitals and other properties in the area, by way of an annual grand waterborne procession, up until 1852.

Upper Watergate Stairs and Causeway

These stairs were much used by watermen to row lightermen and stevedores to and from Deptford Upper and Lower Tiers. The fare for a single journey was sixpence.

Deptford Supply Reserve Depôt (Deptford Dockyard)

In an attempt to strengthen England's power against possible hostilities with France and Spain, Henry VIII built some 40 warships at his dockyards at Woolwich and Deptford. The Deptford Royal Dockyard, which occupied the site seen in this part of the panorama, was completed around 1520. The early yard was equipped with a basin, or wet-dock – for fitting out ships – and a double dry-dock – for the repair, or construction, of two vessels simultaneously. No other royal dockyard was to be so well equipped until the early years of the following century. Ships built at both Deptford and Woolwich played a vital part in the defeat of the Spanish Armada in 1588. Deptford Dockyard was also the starting point for many voyages of exploration. In 1576 Sir Martin Frobisher sailed from here to try and find a north-east passage to China. The following year Francis Drake left on his voyage around the world, for which he was knighted at Deptford by Queen Elizabeth, in 1581. Drake's ship, the *Pelican* (or *Golden Hinde*), was then laid up at the dockyard as a memorial.

In 1698, Czar Peter the Great worked at the dockyard to gain personal knowledge of shipbuilding techniques. He resided nearby at Sayes Court, home of the diarist John Evelyn. By that time however, Deptford had been surpassed by both Chatham and Portsmouth Royal Dockyards in importance. Insufficient depth of water on the river prevented the building of First Rate warships and the great distance from the sea discouraged the sending of naval ships here for repair. Smaller warships, however, were built in great numbers and the yard was expanded in 1780 and 1796, when it employed over 1000 men. Despite this, the yard later ran into difficulties – it launched no ships between 1827 and 1843 – and finally closed in 1869. Between 1700 and its closure some 190 ships had been built or rebuilt at the yard. During the early 1840s some major improvements were made, including the construction of the two iron-roofed slipway buildings, seen in the panorama, which still remain.

In 1871 the site became the Foreign Cattle Market, operated by the City Corporation, for the importation, slaughter and sale of sheep and cows. The market closed in 1913 and was requisitioned during the Great War as a food supply centre for the services. Part of the site continued to be used by the War Department, as the Supply Reserve Depot, and part was used by Convoy's Ltd, general wharfingers, specialising in the importation of newsprint, rolls of which can be seen on the wharf and in lighters lying alongside. Convoy's subsequently expanded their operations and still operate the wharf, which provides up to date roll-on/roll-off facilities for ships up to 18,000 tons.

War Department Steamer

The War Department operated a special fleet of coasters, part of the so-called 'Woolwich Navy'. Based at the department's headquarters at Woolwich Arsenal, these ships carried guns and munitions, as well as foodstuffs and stores.

Frank Bowen, writing in 1938, found these humble vessels of great interest because: 'For one thing their flag is difficult to identify, a Blue Ensign defaced by gold guns which is not included in most popular books of flags, and for another thing, although they are painted black, with a buff funnel and black top, they do not carry their names painted on their bows like ordinary merchant ships but, man-of-war fashion, in very small letters on the stern which are generally difficult to read. . . . They are manned by an entirely separate service, the personnel generally being entered as boys and promoted through the various grades of Ordinary Seamen, A.B., Second Mate, and Mate to Captain, while below deck the grades are Fireman, Leading Hand, and Driver. They wear a uniform of sorts, and although the discipline is not to be compared with either the Army or the Navy, they are generally men of a very superior, steady type who have a good job and who look after it well. Pensions have only been introduced in comparatively recent years for the officers'.

Royal Victoria Victualling Yard

The Admiralty Victualling Yard was established at Deptford in 1742, when existing storehouses at Little Tower Hill had become inadequate for the needs of a growing Navy. Occupying a site immediately to the north-west of Deptford Dockyard, the Victualling Yard had an eventful early life, suffering a series of major fires between 1748—60. Extensive rebuilding took place in the 1780s and by 1860 the Yard had expanded to cover some 35 acres. At that time the site contained stores for clothing,

food, tobacco and rum, supplying Navy depots abroad. One rum vat alone was said to be capable of supplying up to 32,000 gallons of spirit. In addition there were: slaughterhouses; pickling houses; biscuit, chocolate, mustard and pepper manufactories; brewhouses; sail-lofts; wheelwrights' shop; a coopers' shop and sawmills.

In the panorama can be seen the fine range of Rum Warehouses and offices dating from

1781—89, which still remain. The attractive piered watergate of the same date also survives. The Rum Warehouses, and more massive nineteenth century mills and storehouses — which still survived in the 1930s — were all designed in the architectural style characteristic of Naval Dockyards. The ironclad transit sheds and quayside cranes, since demolished, provided a similar cargo handling function to those in the enclosed docks.

As the largest of the Navy's Home Victualling Establishments — the other two being at Gosport and Plymouth — the Royal Victoria Yard remained operational until 1961. The site later became part of the Greater London Council's showpiece Pepys Estate, the Rum Warehouses being converted into flats and a boat sailing centre.

South Wharf

The panorama frequently presents a picture of interesting contrasts. Here it is dominated by the reefed sails, masts and sprits of two sailing barges moored across the river at the Millwall Barge Roads. The funnel is probably that of the Aberdeen Steam Navigation Company's steam tender *Ich Diene* (see under 'Torrington Arms' and Stairs, on the north bank section). The vessels and crewmen have an air of expectation — perhaps they are awaiting the tide. On the Surrey shore, the regimented open timber storage sheds of Acorn Yard, Surrey Commercial Docks, mark the skyline. The white painted riverside buildings and associated jetty in the middle-distance, however, had nothing to do with the normal trading activities of the great commercial port.

In 1881, the Metropolitan Asylum Board had established two hospital ships at Greenwich Reach for the isolation of smallpox patients. The ships were reberthed at Long Reach

in 1884, and were later replaced by a hospital, on the Kentish marshes. The Board acquired South Wharf in 1883 and provided accommodation for patients awaiting transference to Long Reach by its fleet of ambulance steamers. These had distinctive black funnels with brown bands, and long deck saloons, with frosted glass windows. The building on the left accommodated medical staff and those on the right had beds for 24 patients. Between 1884 and 1929, when the London County Council took over the operation, some 140,000 patients, staff and visitors had been carried from South Wharf and the smaller North Wharf, Blackwall, to Long Reach.

With the decline of smallpox and the greater use of motor ambulance services, the steamer operations declined and ceased altogether in the early 1930s. South Wharf, however, was to have a continued association with the LCC as a base for the London Fire Brigade's fire floats.

Trinity Wharf

Much of the Rotherhithe waterfront, like the Surrey Docks behind it, was associated with the handling of timber. At Trinity Wharf timber can be seen piled high on the quayside and being discharged from barges by steam cranes. Although the wharf appears to be dominated by the softwood trade, it also handled other cargoes such as hardwoods, paper, wood pulp boards, waxes and canned fruits coming in by barge.

The parapet to the earlier building on the left, bears a well weathered painted sign which states that the proprietors of this sufferance wharf are 'LIGHTERMEN WHARFINGERS AND CARTAGE CONTRACTORS' – 'STEAM AND SAILING VESSELS DISCHARGED AND LOADED'.

Each of the roof sections of this six-bayed building is ventilated to help with the seasoning of stored timber. Behind this building can be seen blocks of workers' flats in Rotherhithe Street and, behind those, the tower of Holy Trinity Church.

In the 1930s, A G Linney described Holy Trinity as an 'ivied church . . . where much of the burial ground has been asphalted over, and mouldering, white tombstones face the children at their play above the bones of many a stout sea captain and humble seaman of the Port of London'.

The Trinity Wharf Company had operated on this site since the late-nineteenth century. The wharf, together with the church behind, were destroyed during the blitz of 1940. Whilst the wharf was rebuilt, from 1947, the church was left in ruins.

Timber Rafts

Off both Trinity Wharf and Durand's Wharf were moorings for large rafts of floating timber. Heavy baulks of wood, discharged from ships in the Surrey Commercial Docks, would be formed into rafts and towed here and stored afloat to await landing. With strong river tides, it was important to secure the rafted timbers in the safest possible way. This was done by skilled workers, known as 'rafters', who lashed the timbers together with heavy iron staples and ropes.

Durand's Wharf

To the north of Trinity Wharf lay Durand's Wharf, whose river frontage was far more extensive. Like Trinity Wharf, however, Durand's Wharf specialised in the handling of timber.

Nelson Dry Dock

The building of ships, first in wood and later in iron, was a major industry on the Thames from the medieval period up until 1911. In that year London's longstanding inability to compete with lower cost shipyards on the Tyne and Clyde led to the closure of the last major shipyard, belonging to the great Thames Ironworks and Shipbuilding Company at Bow Creek. Closely associated with shipbuilding, historically, was the provision of repair facilities for shipowners. Unlike shipbuilding however, ship repairing was to continue as a major employer, its fortunes directly associated with those of the working port itself.

In 1937 there were some fifteen dry dock facilities for ships on the Thames, between Tilbury and Nelson Dry Dock, twenty-five miles upriver. On the Nelson Dock site ships had been built by a variety of famous London builders – the Taylors; Randall and Brent; Bilbe and Perry – from the mid-seventeenth century until around 1870. Ship repairing, however, was continued by the Nelson Dock Company and then, from the late 1880s to 1968, by Mills and Knight.

On the left-hand side of the photograph can be seen the funnel and superstructure of the Middlesbrough registered ship, SS *Dona*

Flora, behind the dry dock's iron caisson. The dry dock dates from around 1790 and was extended and altered in the late nineteenth century. Lying across the front of the yard is the General Steam Navigation Company's ship, SS *Peregrine*, which is presumably awaiting dry docking. To the right, behind the stern quarters of the SS *Peregrine*, can be seen a smaller ship which has been drawn up on the 'patent' slipway, for work on the hull. Beyond the slipway can be seen the hydraulic engine house which operated the carriage which pulled the ships up out of the water. The 'patent' slipway dates from

the late 1850s and the engine house was in existence by 1868. To the left, the building with the distinctive cupola is the mid-eighteenth century Nelson Dock House. The large range of sheds which can be seen are not part of the dockyard, but timber storage sheds at Acorn Yard, Surrey Commercial Docks. To the right of the shipyard can be seen part of Columbia Wharf, an early example of a silo granary, dating from the 1860s.

The dry dock, slipway, engine house, shipwright's building and Nelson House still survive and it is hoped that the site's long association with shipbuilding and repairing will be marked by the establishment of a small heritage centre.

Bellamy's Wharf

Bellamy's Wharf & Dock Co Ltd operated two extensive and adjoining wharves in Rotherhithe. Part of Bellamy's Wharf, with one of its goose-neck electric quay cranes, can just be seen on the left of the photograph, whilst King and Queen Wharf can be seen on the right. During the 1930s both wharves were listed as being licensed to store dried fruits, sugar, bulk grain and general cargoes.

During the late eighteenth and early nineteenth century the site had been occupied by Mestaers Shipyard.

SS *Shaftesbury*

Owned and operated under the British flag by the Alexander Shipping Company, the dimensions of this steam ship – 370 feet long and a gross tonnage of 4284 – show how effective Bellamy's Jetty was at accommodating sizeable vessels. It is interesting to note that the *Shaftesbury* would have been too large to have entered St Katharine's Dock, London Dock, or the East India Dock. A grab can be seen discharging what is probably Argentinian wheat into awaiting lighters via a hopper. The ship's derricks are also discharging cargo overside to barges.

Bellamy's Jetty

A number of upriver wharves had extensive jetties, but few could match the facilities offered at Bellamy's Wharf. Here, a 350-foot long jetty allowed large ships which could not be handled in the upper docks to be loaded and discharged at all states of the tide. On the reinforced concrete jetty were nine electric and hydraulic cranes capable of loading and unloading ships, as well as barges, which were able to moor inside the jetty.

King and Queen Wharf

This large, early twentieth century, warehouse was also known as Bellamy's Granaries. As its name implies, it concentrated on the grain side of Bellamy's Wharf & Dock Company's activities. It offered some of the most extensive facilities for handling and storing grain on London's riverfront – indeed it was the only riverside wharf equipped for the handling of bulk grain. There had been an earlier granary here in the 1850s, and in the 1790s the site was occupied by a timber yard, a boat yard and King and Queen Stairs.

Bull Head Dock Wharf

Tucked away behind Bellamy's Jetty, was a small general wharf with its own barge dock. The barge dock occupied the site of a historic dry dock, which had belonged to the shipwrights J & R B Brown in the 1850s. In the 1830s it had been Beatson's Yard and in the 1790s it had belonged to Mr Woolcombe. It was at Beatson's Yard that the gallant warship, the 'Téméraire', immortalised in Turner's famous painting, was broken up in 1838–39.

Surrey Commercial Wharf

To the right of the photograph can be seen part of Gerhard and Hey's Wharf, which handled furs, skins, essential oils and general cargoes. As well as larger quayside cranes, this wharf had a small steam crane to unload the barges which delivered their cargoes here.

Thames Tunnel Mills

This massive building, which is named after the nearby Thames Tunnel — by Sir Marc Isambard Brunel and opened in 1843 — dates from the late nineteenth century. The earliest part is that with the stone cornices which dates from the 1870s, together with the chimneyed boiler and engine house alongside. The mill on the left is later, as is the granary building, to the right of the boiler house. It was operated by White, Tomkins and Courage, millers, who warehoused and manufactured a wide range of foodstuffs. Flaked rice, tapioca flakes and cooked flaked maize were made for the home and export markets, besides products for the London brewing industry. Having closed in the early 1970s the main part of the mill was subsequently acquired by the London and Quadrant Housing Association, whose imaginative conversion into flats has won much praise since their completion in 1983.

St Mary, Rotherhithe

The parish church of Rotherhithe, which still survives, stands on the site of a medieval church which had fallen into disrepair by the beginning of the eighteenth century. Rebuilding of the church began in 1714; the tower, which provides a noticeable riverside landmark, being added in 1747. Carvings in the sanctuary, said to be by Grinling Gibbons were removed from the earlier church. The church abounds in memorials and other links with the sea. Christopher Jones, captain of the *Mayflower* which carried the Pilgrim Fathers to America, was buried in the churchyard in 1662. Also buried there is 'Prince Lee Boo, son of Abba Thule, Rupack or King of Island of Coo-roo-ran, one of the Pelew Islands', who died of smallpox, at Rotherhithe, in the 1780s. Memorials in the church include one to Joseph Wade, King's Carver at Deptford and Woolwich Royal Dockyards, who died in 1743.

Carr's Engineering Works

The small building to the left of Hope Wharf was occupied by G Carr and Sons, barge builders, engineers and chainmakers, during the 1930s. In the 1890s it was known variously as Hope Anchor Works and St Mary's Ironworks. During the 1970s it was occupied by the towage firm of W E White and Sons and is now a craft glassblowing workshop – a sign of the changing nature of this part of Rotherhithe.

Hope Wharf

The site of this late nineteenth-century warehouse was occupied by J Goddard's open coal wharf and depot in the 1850s. The warehouse was later occupied by L Farrel and then passed into the hands of A J Gardiner and Sons, general wharfingers. It still survives and is generally known by its more recent name of Hope Sufferance Wharf. On the landward side an earlier nineteenth century granary building, which also remains, can be seen. The open space to the right of Hope Wharf is now a small public garden offering good views of the river and the wharf's restored electric wall crane, which was made by East Ferry Road Engineering Works, on the Isle of Dogs, in 1930, and could lift 12½ cwt.

Bombay Wharf

These late nineteenth century warehouses, with unusual Dutch gables, were built on the site of a timber barge building shed. In 1937 they were being used by G and H Green, wharfingers, who had a small quayside electric crane to help with the loading and unloading of barges. The building on the left still stands.

East India Wharf

These two mid nineteenth century granary buildings have an interesting history. In 1857 the one on the left was W Lyons Granary and that on the right W W Landell's Granary. Between the two warehouses was an open barge building yard. Thirty years later, both buildings were being operated, as a granary, by John Dudin and Sons. During the 1930s the wharf was operated by British Bluefries Wharfage and Transport Ltd.

Lying off India Wharf is one of W M J Alexander's smaller steam tugs, the *Sundial*. Built in 1898, primarily for craft towage, this vessel was sometimes engaged in the movement of ships up to the Hay's Wharf Group of warehouses, above Tower Bridge. In 1938 she was acquired by Silvertown Services and renamed the *Silverdial*. This tug was later lost on war service in Portland Harbour.

Beard's Wharf and Carr's Wharf

Barge building yards had existed on this site since at least the 1850s. Beard's Wharf, owned by the lighterage firm of T W Beard & Co, was used for barge repairing during the 1930s. In 1900 it had belonged to Smith Bros, barge builders. Carr's Wharf was occupied by G Carr and Sons, engineers and barge builders. A large swim-headed hatch barge is on the blocks, apparently undergoing the fitting of new ceilings. In 1900 this yard had belonged to the barge-building firm of Ward & Sons.

Both Beard's and Carr's works were later jointly operated as part of Prince's Ironworks. Beard's built a number of lighters for the Thames Steam Tug and Lighterage Company.

Elephant Stairs and the 'Torbay' Public House

This historic waterman's stair, with the old houses in Elephant Lane beyond, and the 'Torbay' alongside, represent a survival of the early Rotherhithe waterfront.

Prince's Wharf

This extensive warehouse was built on the site of a large timber framed barge and boat-building yard, which existed in the late 1850s. From early on, it had been occupied by Gillman and Spencer and was used for the warehousing of bagged and loose cereals.

Gordon's Wharf

This was another late nineteenth century warehouse, operated by Gillman and Spencer, used for cereals. It was linked, across Prince's Stairs, to Prince's Wharf and also contained a mill. Like Prince's Wharf it had replaced older premises such as a sailmaker's, ship chandler's, and mastmaker's, characteristic of Rotherhithe's early waterfront.

In the foreground can be seen the iron sailing barge *Barbara Jean*, owned by R & W Paul, of Ipswich. Built at Brightlingsea in 1924, she was one of the largest barges ever constructed, capable of carrying around 260 tons. She was one of sixteen Thames sailing barges to cross the Channel for the evacuation of Dunkirk in 1940, and was blown up and abandoned on the beach there.

Abbot's Wharf and Cannon Wharf

The range of granary buildings west of Gordon's Wharf show something of the complex pattern of wharf holdings on London's river. Abbot's Wharf, the tall thin building immediately to the right of Gordon's Wharf, was owned by A H & E Foster, whilst Cannon Wharf, to its right, was owned by Gillman and Spencer, the owners of Prince's and Gordon's Wharves. Both buildings date from the late nineteenth century — Abbot's Wharf having been built on the site of an earlier granary and Cannon Wharf on the sites of a ship's blockmaker's premises and a flour wharf.

Rotherhithe Wharf and Mathews Wharf

Rotherhithe Wharf — the wider building with the broken pediment — was also owned by A H & E Foster and was used for the storage of the seeds, grain, corn and cereals. During the 1850s a steam flour mill had stood on the site. On the right of the photograph is Mathew's Wharf, another granary building, also owned by Foster's. Both buildings are late nineteenth century.

As with many other granary buildings, those to the west of Gordon's Wharf were equipped with only 5 cwt capacity cranes to handle the relatively light bagged cargoes coming in by barge. The tall granary building, between the two wharves, was originally known as Fountain Wharf.

Yardley's Wharf

Another late nineteenth century granary building, occupied by Yardley's Wharf Ltd, for the storage of cereal products. This granary is somewhat unusual in that a large electric crane has been added to supplement the simple hoists above the loading doors.

Cochin Wharf

This smaller nineteenth century warehouse, used for storing cereals, was another belonging to A H & E Foster Ltd.

Pocock's Barge Yard

Henry Pocock, barge builder, had occupied a number of the riverside buildings west of Cochin Wharf for many years. Another of his premises, which advertises him as 'Barge Builder' with 'Barges to Let', can be seen closer to King's Stairs. Such ramshackle buildings high above the foreshore at low tide, offered great difficulties for barge repair work.

'Jolly Waterman' Public House

The building with the two long windows onto the riverfront was an historic tavern which remained in use until the early 1930s.

Like many of the buildings on this stretch of the waterfront, the house that had been the 'Jolly Waterman' survived into the early 1960s. Most of the buildings here date from the mid eighteenth century and would have been well known to James McNeill Whistler, who depicted Rotherhithe in one of the famous 'Thames Set' of etchings. By the 1950s this range of buildings, like the Limehouse riverfront, had acquired a romantic attachment for the *avant-garde* — Anthony Armstrong Jones lived here and Princess Margaret was said to have been a frequent visitor.

Kings Stairs and the 'Dover Castle' Public House

Another waterman's stairs with a late nineteenth century public house alongside, to the right. Stairs and public houses were normally associated on London's waterfront – the latter earning a busy trade from watermen, lightermen, other port workers and travellers.

The building to the left of the stairs is the only building shown on this photograph to survive. It is now occupied by Braithwaite and Dean, the only lighterage firm still based in the area covered by the panorama.

Pace's Wharf

George Pace was another barge builder, owner and hirer on this stretch of the river.

Braithwaite and Dean's Wharf

Established in the early 1900s, Braithwaite and Dean were bargebuilders, repairers and bargeowners. The premises on the extreme right also belonged to them. It adjoined the 'Angel' public house (not seen here), now the only other survivor of this stretch of early riverfront.

MV *Apollinaris*

Dutch built and registered, this modest short sea trader of 148 tons gross reflects much of the maritime tradition of her home country. Built of steel in 1924, with a diesel engine, this ship also had an auxiliary gaff rigged mainsail. It was owned by H Mulder, of Gronigen, who operated a sister vessel, *Apollinaris II*, built in 1927.

On the bargebed, ships' painters are busy taking advantage of the tide, scraping and blacking up the hull of the boat.

Lucas and Spencer's Wharf

This wharf was also known as Apollinaris Wharf, which specialised in importing the mineral water of that name from Germany. Crates of mineral water can be seen being unloaded by the large wall crane from the auxiliary sailing vessel *Apollinaris*.

The warehouse, which has a graceful architectural façade, dates from around 1870. One interesting original feature of this building is the double chimneyed, corrugated-iron boilerhouse between the main fourth-floor loading doors. This contained 'patent' gas boilers which supplied steam to operate the four small wall cranes. Whereas coal and coke fired boilers — employed in the operation of steam cranes and steam-engine generated hydraulic cranes — had to be located in brick vaults, gas boilers were permitted to be attached to the outside of buildings. With the coming of a public supply of hydraulic power in 1883, and later, electric power, many of the earlier 'in-house' attempts to provide power for warehouse cranes became obsolete. The wharf occupied the site of an earlier granary, a guano wharf and the 'Lion and Castle' public house. The building was later acquired by Chambers Wharf and Cold Stores Ltd and was used for warehousing fresh and refrigerated foodstuffs. It was demolished during the mid-1970s.

Diesel Tug *Orient*

This craft tug was built around 1894 for Page Son and East. It was later owned by the Thames Steam Tug and Lighterage Company before passing into the ownership of the firm of Harry Lane. In the 1930s her original steam plant was replaced by a National diesel engine.

Cherry Garden Pier and Stairs

Both the pier and the earlier waterman's stairs are named after a nearby seventeenth century pleasure garden popular with Londoners. Samuel Pepys visited here in June 1664 and wrote 'to Greenwich . . . and so to the Cherry Garden, and then by water singing finely to the bridge and there landed'.

At the junction of the Lower Pool and Upper Pool, the pier offered splendid views of the river and its busy traffic. The pier, owned by the Port of London Authority, was itself the focus of much activity. It was off the pier that ships bound up through Tower Bridge had to hoist their signal pennants and blow their whistles to alert the Bridge Master. The skilled River Pilots who helped captains navigate ships and colliers on the tricky river above London Bridge were also based here. A public house on the south side of Bermondsey Wall was called the 'Ship and Pilot'. There was also a mooring nearby for London County Council fire floats. Earlier on the pier had been a stopping-off point for passenger steamers.

Cherry Garden Wharf and Farrand's Wharf

Both Cherry Garden Wharf, immediately to the right of the pier, and Farrand's Wharf were operated by the local wharfingers, Gardiner and Tidy. Cherry Garden Wharf had very limited facilities — open wharfage and a small electric crane — for handling general cargoes, like the oil drums seen here.

Farrand's Wharf, however, is an imposing mid nineteenth century warehouse, mainly handling bagged flour and foodstuffs. The wharf was operated in the 1850s by Messrs Young and Raymond, as a granary. The wharf lacked any form of jetty — barges coming directly alongside to have the relatively light bags unloaded by the simple overhead hoists. As with many other flour and granary warehouses on the Rotherhithe and Bermondsey waterfront, the walls by the loading doors have been discoloured by powdery foodstuffs. The large warehouse seen behind, on the south side of Rotherhithe Wall, was part of Farrand's Wharf and was linked to the riverside buildings by a catwalk.

Powell's Wharf

This wharf was operated by Caledonian Wharfage, handling mostly sugar and confectionery. Dating from the mid nineteenth century, the buildings had originally been granaries operated by two separate wharfingers. Young and Raymond, wharfingers and cornfactors, operated the easternmost one and Begbie and Young, also cornfactors, occupied the western building. Besides lighters, coasters also came alongside to be discharged.

Fountain Stairs

Here can be seen another waterman's stairs, continuing its historic course through a much later building. The stone flagged causeway which leads onto the foreshore, enabled river travellers to reach the stairs, relatively dry shod, at low tide.

Fountain Stairs Wharf

Dating from the same period as Powell's Wharf, these granary buildings were also occupied by Caledonian Wharfage in the 1930s. Before that the wharf had also been known as Darnell's Granaries, named after their owners, W & J R Darnell. During the 1850s the wharf was occupied by Begbie and Young, cornfactors. Originally the only method of unloading barges would have been by manual hoists, although warehouse 'B' has had a small wall crane added and warehouse 'C', a large electric wall crane.

Darnell's Wharf

Alongside Fountain Stairs Wharf was another granary of around the same date. Darnell's retained ownership of this building until 1930, when it was transferred to Bennett's Haulage, Warehousing & Wharfage Co Ltd. As a result the wharf was also known as Bennett's Lower Wharf.

Fountain Dock

This small dock yard, operated by Mills and Knight, ship repairers up until 1935, represents a very interesting survival. Shipbuilding, or repairing, had been carried on here since the eighteenth century. In the 1790s the yard was occupied by Smith & Co, and in the 1830s by the firm of Westlake. During the 1850s the yard was owned by Williams and Sons, when the site included a slipway, between the two sheds seen here, and a large dry dock, at the eastern end towards Darnell's Wharf. The timber shed, on the left, was a shipwright's store, with saw-pits under in 1857. The later corrugated-iron building on the right probably dates from the turn of this century. By the 1890s, when Mills and Knight occupied the site, the slipway was in disuse, replaced by a gridiron on the foreshore for the repair of coasters and barges. The large hand crane on the quayside would have been built to facilitate repair work on vessels lying on the gridiron, much of which could only have taken place at low tide.

Fountain Hole Barge Tier

Moored in the channel can be seen a number of lighters belonging to the Humphery & Grey Lighterage Company. Just behind is their steam tug *Lady Sybil*, built in 1913, later operated by the Tilbury Contracting & Dredging Co Ltd. To the right are fully laden timber barges from the Surrey Commercial Docks. Behind them sheeted lighters are lying at Bond's Wharf.

Bond's Wharf

Two more mid nineteenth century grain warehouses, known as Bond's Granary in the 1890s. During the 1930s the wharf was operated by the firm of Harold Bellingham, wharfingers, who, from the appearance of the building, must still have been handling bagged foodstuffs.

Chamber's Wharves

Immediately to the west of Bond's Wharf were Chamber's Wharves. Operated by Chamber's Wharf and Cold Stores Ltd, these wharves had recently been known as Montreal Wharf – occupied by John Dudin and Sons, wharfingers and lightermen – and Sunderland Wharf, occupied by T Addis and Sons, wharfingers. Between the two late nineteenth century warehouses a new wharf, which still survives, and cold store can be seen in the course of construction.

Whilst Chamber's wharves handled general cargoes – including lead, glues, beans, peas, rice, seeds, nuts and other produce – they specialised in canned goods and frozen foods, particularly meat.

The deepwater jetty, which could handle large ships, has an interesting range of cranes, including two 10-ton electric cranes, a 10-ton Scotch derrick and a smaller steam crane. The jetty was later extended still

further. By the early 1960s, when the whole wharf had been rebuilt in brick and reinforced concrete, the company could advertise its services as providing 'steamer berths; specialists in storage of dried and canned foods especially frozen foods; quick and efficient handling; direct discharge from ship and craft to cold store; customs facilities; transport available; night delivery service; equipped for meat cutting'.

East Lane Wharf

This large open wharf belonged to Bermondsey Borough Council and was used as a refuse wharf. Rubbish was shot into lighters through the three large chutes, for dumping downriver for land reclamation. The wharf had earlier been used by Bermondsey Vestry for the same purpose. In the mid nineteenth century the site was occupied by the historic Fore and Aft Dry Dock and a coal wharf.

London Grist Mills

This mid nineteenth century corn mill was occupied by the London Grist Mill Company, who had been on the site since the late 1800s. In the 1850s it had been T Groves & Sons' granary.

Seaborne Coal Wharf

The use of this wharf for handling imported coal from the Tyne and Wear dates from the late nineteenth century. During the 1850s the site had been occupied by a boat builder and an importer of barrel hoops. During the late 1930s the wharf mainly handled animal bones imported for the manufacture of glue.

Reed's Lower Wharf

Another late nineteenth century granary building, occupied by H T Reed and Sons, wharfingers, which stood on the site of an earlier boatbuilder's premises.

Deverell's Wharf

This modified mid nineteenth century warehouse was used for warehousing foodstuffs and general cargoes. In the 1850s it was used as a granary by Messrs Swayne and Bovill. Immediately behind this stretch of waterfront, up until the mid nineteenth century, was the infamous Jacob's Island. Formed by the rambling watercourses of the River Neckinger, Jacob's Island, with its horrendous housing and sanitary conditions, was immortalised in Charles Dickens' *Oliver Twist* as the scene of Bill Sikes' death.

Uveco Wharf

This recent, and very utilitarian, wharf was occupied by Spillers Ltd and used for milling and the manufacture of dog biscuits. The grain elevator discharged from barges into the large brick and concrete silo, for milling in the building behind. The mill closed in 1983.

Reed's Wharf

These mid nineteenth century granary and mill buildings were occupied by H T Reed and Sons, whose family had owned granaries here since at least the late eighteenth century. The wharf sat over Mill Stairs, which allowed river workers and travellers access to the river. During the 1850s Reed's handled both coal and corn at this wharf. After the last war the wharf was operated by Wheat Sheaf Mills Ltd, who brought wheat and barley in by barge, and sent out milled flour by both barge and lorry.

Meriton's Wharf

Named after an eighteenth century granary, the building – which turns the eastern corner of St Saviour's Dock – dates from the early 1890s. Built by Seth Taylor, grain merchant, it was re-christened New Concordia Wharf after Concordia, Kansas City, Missouri. The wharf operated as a grain and seed mill until 1934, when it was sold to the Butler's Wharf Company. By 1937 the large wall cranes had been added and the building leased to British Bluefries Wharfage, who used it for warehousing tea and other commodities.

Closed in the early 1970s, the wharf has been converted since 1982 to award-winning apartments.

St Saviour's Dock

This is the former mouth of one of London's lost rivers, the Neckinger. The river's lower course became St Saviour's Dock, a tidal inlet stretching from Dockhead to the Thames. By the 1930s the Dock contained an interesting mix of warehouses, granaries and flour and seed mills, dating from around 1840–1900, most of which rose majestically from the piled waterfront itself. On the right can be seen the recently built Butler's Wharf Extension warehouse.

With the combined problems of tide, mud and the crowding of craft on the riverfront, lightermen who brought their barges here had little love for this patch of water. A G Linney graphically described their problems in the 1930s: 'The passageway grows narrower and darker and is no more than a chasm until you have to strike inland towards Dockhead which marks the limit of that narrow and busy cut . . . where two dozen warehouses are closely packed against one another. Up this cut creep lighters with hardly room to pass each other. Looking down St Saviour's Dock from its end, but the tiniest strip of sky shows between the grim walls. For a good part of the way barges lie disconsolate upon the mud, for St Saviour's is navigable in its length of 300 yards only for an hour each side of high water'.

More recently, however, the evocative buildings and enclosed waterspace of the dock have attracted a very different clientele of luxury apartment dwellers.

Butler's Wharf Extension

The waterfront and warehouses of Shad Thames, the area between St Saviour's Dock and Courage's Brewery, were dominated by the activities of the Butler's Wharf Company. By the 1930s the Company was engaged in a wide range of activities including the importation of rubber, spices, fruit, colonial and European general produce. Extensive warehousing existed for wines and spirits

and for the blending and repacking of tea. The Butler's Wharf Extension building, which turned the western corner of St Saviour's Dock, was a modern warehouse complex of reinforced concrete and brick built in 1922. It incorporated three powerful electric wall cranes, which could luff out to discharge directly from ships and barges. This warehouse continued in use until 1972,

when the company ceased to operate its wharves.

The mid nineteenth century warehouse, to the right, is one of the earlier granary buildings which once lined the Bermondsey waterfront. Civil engineering works to the piled quayside can be seen in progress.

Horselydown New Stairs

The site of this ancient waterman's stairs is clearly indicated by the passageway between Butler's Wharf warehouse, on the left, and Cole's Wharf, on the right.

Cole's Wharf

This granary building – of mid nineteenth century appearance – with its six-storey façade, contrasts visibly with some of the more massive warehouses belonging to Butler's Wharf. Granary buildings often had lower floor heights than general cargo warehouses. During the 1930s this wharf was operated by Addis and Keen Ltd who handled seeds, grain, cereals and flour. An elevator can be seen discharging from the outermost of the two barges, whose 'crew' of pigeons and gulls are being well fed! The pediment of the building seems to have been rebuilt and the brickwork of the whole façade is remarkably clean, compared to those alongside.

To the right of Cole's Wharf main building is a smaller mid nineteenth century granary. The brickwork around the loading doors has been stained white by flour and grain. Cole's Wharf was later absorbed into the Butler's Wharf Company, who continued to use it for the grain trade.

Butler's Wharf

Seen here are Butler's Wharf 'D' and 'E' warehouses, built by John Aird & Son in 1871–73 to the designs of James Tolley and Daniel Dale. Of considerable architectural merit, warehouse 'E' has rusticated quoins and bracketed cornices supporting a pediment. To the east were the matching 'A' to 'C' warehouses, originally separated from those seen here by a central pedimented warehouse with a cartway through to the quayside from Shad Thames. Like the Hay's Wharf warehouses upriver, these buildings were of composite construction, with brick vaulted basements, partial 'fireproof' floors and both iron and timber columns, as well as wrought iron roof trusses. It seems likely that the work of 1871–83 may have involved a certain amount of rebuilding – in 1865 a new block of building had dramatically collapsed into the river.

When constructed, these buildings comprised the largest wharf on the river.

They were linked to the Butler's Wharf Company's landward warehouses across Shad Thames by overhead iron cartways. H M Tomlinson aptly captured the atmosphere of this street when he described it as 'a cobbled track confined by lofty buildings, and these connect across the chasm in numerous bridges as frail as spider-webbing'. Having closed in 1972, the warehouses are now the subject of major restoration and conversion by Conran Roche.

Anchor Brewhouse

Immediately to the west of Butler's Wharf warehouse can be seen the variegated, but imposing, riverside façades of Courage's Anchor Brewhouse. Courage had been brewing beer here since 1789, but a fire in 1892 led to much of the brewery being rebuilt by the architects Inskip and McKenzie.

The rebuilding of the brewhouse was completed in 1895 – the date being clearly visible on the stone plaque on the gable of

Tower Bridge

Tower Bridge

image

Tower Bridge

image

Tower Bridge

image

Tower Bridge

image

Tower Bridge Wharf

This late nineteenth century warehouse specialised in the handling of imported hides and skins from the East Indies for the nearby leather trade of Bermondsey. By the time of the panorama it formed part of the Hays Wharf Group, whose trading activities dominated the whole riverfront between Tower Bridge and London Bridge.

Dredger *Hope*

Steam bucket dredgers like the *Hope* were kept busy in the port, maintaining deep water in river channels and at moorings. Built in 1901 at Paisley for the Board of Trade, the *Hope* was self-propelled. By the 1930s she was owned by the London firm R G Odell, who used her in conjunction with their *Hopper No 19*, which conveyed the dredged spoil downriver to be dumped. The *Hope* was still operational in the 1950s.

Mark Brown's Wharf

This group of warehouses were one of a number of sufferance wharves created in the eighteenth century on the Southwark waterfront. The largest warehouse of brick and reinforced concrete bears the date 1906. To the west are two late nineteenth century warehouses. Mark Brown's Wharf specialised in the handling of a wide variety of provisions and general cargoes from Europe. In 1929 these warehouses were acquired by the Hay's Wharf group who were to add the large cold store, for dairy produce, seen behind the 1906 warehouse.

SS *Baltrader*

Built in 1919 and owned by the United Baltic Corporation, this ship was a frequent visitor to the Hays Wharf Group, carrying food produce from Europe. Like many other Baltic traders using this stretch of river, this ship also had limited passenger carrying facilities. After May 1937 the ship was transferred to Hull, and was sunk by a mine on 9 November 1940 with the loss of two crew. Casks of wine, thought to have come from this vessel, were washed up at Margate in October and November 1941.

Mark Brown's Wharf

The late nineteenth century warehouse, on the left of the photograph, is the westernmost end of the one seen in the previous section of the panorama. Alongside it is a provisions warehouse dated 1914. On the wharf can be seen two of the six modern electric quayside cranes which delivered cargo to and from Mark Brown's four warehouses.

MV _Lech_

Owned by the Polish British Steamship Company, with a gross registered tonnage of 1,568, and built in 1934 by Swan Hunter on Tyneside. Registered at Gydnia in Poland, she was another regular trader to the Upper Pool, carrying foodstuffs.

Pickle Herring Wharf

It is uncertain whether this wharf owed its name to an early trade in pickled fish. What is certain is that the place-name of 'Pyckleherying' was in use in the mid sixteenth century and that a Pickleherring Wharf existed by 1661. The wharf was created a sufferance wharf during the early nineteenth century, although the warehouse buildings seen here date from the end of the century. Pickle Herring Wharf eventually became part of the Hay's Wharf Group.

St Olave's Wharf

This mid nineteenth century warehouse was also a sufferance wharf. Operated by Beresford and Co, in 1937 it specialised in the handling of hides, skins, leather and general cargoes. The wharf was ill-equipped compared to the neighbouring ones belonging to the Hay's Wharf Group: its lack of any quayside limiting its cranage facilities to wall cranes suitable only for use on barges. The building was demolished in the 1950s.

Pickle Herring Stairs

This ancient waterman's stair sat over the southern end of the disused Tower Subway. The Subway was operational from 1870–97, originally with cable hauled trams carrying 14 people, and latterly as a foot tunnel only.

Stanton's Wharf

Alongside Pickle Herring Stairs, Stanton's Wharf has been demolished to make way for a new warehouse for the Hay's Wharf Group. The large, late nineteenth century provisions warehouse in the background was partly occupied by Wigan Richardson's Cold Stores Ltd.

Immediately west of Stanton's Wharf was Symon's Wharf, also owned by the Hay's Wharf Group, which was demolished at the same time. Beyond this was a building known as Gun and Shot and Griffin's Wharves, the only site between London Bridge and Tower Bridge which Hay's Wharf was eventually unable to acquire. It was operated by the Union Cold Storage Company, who retained it until its closure at the end of the 1960s.

Wilson's Wharf

During the mid nineteenth century this wharf became part of the Hay's Wharf Group. The warehouse bears the date 1868 and was part of the company's great rebuilding scheme. Hay's Wharf transferred their coffee and cocoa operations here from Cotton's Wharf, and the wharf also handled dried fruit and provisions. It was here that the company first operated a wine and spirit bottling department.

MV *Sibier*

This USSR registered diesel ship was built and engined in Leningrad in 1929. Another frequent visitor to the Hay's Wharf Group, the *Sibier* carried food produce from Leningrad in the Gulf of Finland, and Murmansk in the Barents Sea. With a length of 333 feet and a gross tonnage of 3,787 she exemplified the remarkable handling facilities of the Upper Pool. Within a few years, however, the ship was to be sunk in the Gulf of Finland by German aircraft.

Hay's Wharf

Built on the site of an eighteenth century sufferance wharf, the buildings seen here were constructed in 1856–57. Although the warehouse was permitted to handle all cargoes, except tobacco, it specialised in handling provisions and tea. Ships and barges, which had transhipped their cargoes from the lower docks, were discharged by electric quayside cranes.

Originally known as Beale's Wharf this was the first riverside warehouse to have its own hydraulic power supply, generated by two horizontal steam engines acting through an accumulator. At least five other nearby warehouses had their own hydraulic power supply by 1883, when the London Hydraulic Power Company introduced a public supply.

Hay's Dock

One of the most remarkable features of the great rebuilding of Hay's Wharf was the provision of this long and narrow dock, for the greater accommodation of sailing ships and barges. The warehouses, which rise dramatically above the dock's very narrow quay, were built in 1856–57. Along with the neighbouring Hay's Wharf and Humphery's Wharf warehouses, they were built by Sir William Cubitt, to the designs of the architects, William Snooke and Henry Stock. The buildings provided an early and rare attempt – in the Port of London at least – to provide partial fireproofing, by means of alternating floors of brick jack arches, on cast-iron beams and columns, and timber ones, on iron columns.

The dock is now the centrepiece of a prestigious office development – London Bridge City – which has retained its façade, but infilled the water and roofed it over, with glass.

Humphery's Wharf

Despite the attempt to provide fire protection at the new Hay's Wharf warehouses, the great Tooley Street Fire of 1861 destroyed buildings to the east of Cotton's Wharf. The western side of Hay's Dock, together with Humphery's Wharf, which bears the date of 1858, were severely damaged and were rebuilt in facsimile with the insurance money.

SS *Baltallinn*

This London registered steam ship, owned by the United Baltic Corporation, was much engaged in carrying food produce from Tallin in Estonia. Built in 1920 – at Troon, as the *Starling* – she was torpedoed in September 1941, with the loss of seven crew.

Cotton's Wharf

As with a number of the wharves in the Hay's group, this building stood on the site of an eighteenth century sufferance wharf. The wharf had been rebuilt in 1856–57 by Sir William Cubitt, to the designs of William Snooke and Henry Stock. The building was soon to be destroyed, however, by the Tooley Street Fire of 1861, which broke out in a cargo of jute being stored here. After the fire the buildings were rebuilt as before, but the façade shows evidence of more recent alterations to the fourth storey windows. Further alterations took place as a result of war damage and conversion to a cold store. As with other warehouses hereabouts, many of the 'No Smoking' signs and other wharf notices were written in Russian as well as English.

Chamberlain's Wharf

This fine building, which dates from the 1860s, stood on the site of an earlier sufferance wharf. Like the other Hay's Wharf warehouses, it continued to operate up until the closure of the group's operations in 1969. The three large electric quayside cranes each had a capacity to lift up to 10 tons from ships and barges. Hydraulic wall cranes delivered smaller 'sets' of cargoes from the quay to waiting warehousemen at the separately numbered loading doors, known as 'loop-holes'. The building now forms part of the new London Bridge Hospital.

Hay's Wharf Offices

In 1928 the historic parish church of St Olave's was demolished and the site sold to the Hay's Wharf Group by Bermondsey Borough Council. Three years later the company's new Head Offices, designed by H S Goodhart-Rendel in a distinctive 'continental-modern style, opened on the site. A series of gilded faience reliefs, designed by Frank Dobson, forms a distinctive feature of the riverside façade. Three large sculptured reliefs symbolise Capital, Labour and Commerce, whilst thirty-six smaller ones, which feature aspects of cargo-handling, depict the Chain of Distribution. The building still survives.

Although the building was designed to contain only offices, the ground floor is open to allow lorries to pass to and along the quayside.

Greenwich Reach. Taken in September 1934 from a Thames pleasure steamer, this memorable view looked back towards the Royal Naval College. Two of the distinctive Thames spritsail barges were working down river. The *Whimbrel* (nearest to the camera) was built in 1882 and owned by the London & Rochester Trading Company.

The Complete Riverscape Panorama   North Bank

Aerial photograph, taken in the 1930s, looking down on the Wapping waterfront, between St John's Wharf and Free Trade Wharf. The river was busy with tugs and lighters making their way between the moored ships and extensive network of barge roads. Wapping seemed very much an 'island', with its densely packed warehouses, factories and council dwellings surrounded by water; the river to the south, and the London Dock system to the north.

North Bank
London Bridge to Tower Bridge

Facsimile reproduction
with original annotation.
Each titled block represents a
single dissected folded section.

*Selected Riverscapes (page number)

1* (6)

2* (7)

3* (8)

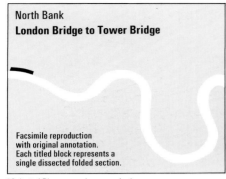

8

9* (12)

10* (13)

11

15* (17)

16

17

18* (18)

22

23* (20)

24* (21)

24A

25

Custom
House
Stairs

Custom House
H.M.S.Harpy

5

Custom House Quay
Galley Dock E Quay
Chester Quay
Brewers Quay

6* (10)

7* (11)

North Bank
Tower Bridge to Union Stairs

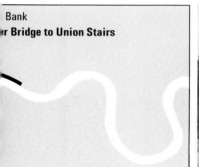

Irongate Wharf

NERAL STEAM NAVIGATION COMPANY LTD

12* (14)

St Katharine's Wharf

13* (15)

St. Katharine Dock Entrance
Harrison's

14* (16)

Hermitage Steam Wharf
Hermitage Steam Wharf

Steam Wharf
Hermitage Stairs
Colonial Wharves
Union Stairs

20

21

North Bank
Union Stairs to Wapping Dock Stairs

St John's Wharf
Morocco Wharf

Eagle Sufferance Wharf
Eagle Wharf
Baltic Wharf
Old Wapping New Stairs

27* (23)

Aberdeen Wharf
Wapping Police Station
St. John's Wharf
ST JOHN'S WHARF

28* (24)

Sun Wharf
Swan Wharf
King Henry's Wharves
Tunnel Pier

29* (25)

Gun Wharves · Wapping Dock Stairs

30

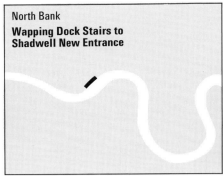

North Bank
Wapping Dock Stairs to Shadwell New Entrance

Wapping Dock Stairs · Lower Gun Wharves

31

Middleton's & St. Bride's Wharves · Foundry Wharf

32

Wharf · Pelican Wharf · Pelican Stairs

37* (26)

Dockmaster's Residence & Office · P.L.A. River Quay

38* (27)

P.L.A. River Quay · Shadwell New Entrance

39

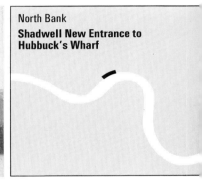

North Bank
Shadwell New Entrance to Hubbuck's Wharf

44* (29)

Free Trade Wharves

45* (30)

Free Trade Wharf

46* (31)

Stone Stairs · Hubbuck's Wharf

47

Ratcliff Cross Stairs · Phoenix Wharf · Ballast Office · Marriage's

51* (32)

Wharf · Roneo Wharf · London Wharf · Crown Mill Wharf · Eagle Wharf

52* (33)

New Sun Wharf · Vanes Wharf · Oporto Wharf

53

Old Sun Wharf

54

's Company Wharf • New Crane Stairs • New

Crane Wharves

NEW CRANE WHARVES

Buchanan's Wharf • Jubilee Wharf • Lushes Wharf • Metropolitan Wharf

METROPOLITAN WHARF

King James Stairs • Queen's

34

35

36

Shadwell New Entrance

Shadwell Dock Stairs • Rotherhithe Tunnel Air Shaft

King Edward VII Memorial Park, Shadwell

FREE WHARF

41

42

43* (28)

Bank
uck's Wharf to
nt's Canal Dock Entrance

Hubbuck's Wharf

HUBBUCK'S WHARF   HUBBUCKS PAINTS

Ratcliff Cross Wharf

TRADE

Lendrum's Wharf

WHARF

48

49

50

F

Regent's Canal Dock Entrance

North Bank
Regent's Canal Dock Entrance to
Limekiln Dock

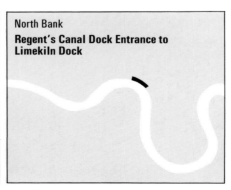
Regent's Canal Dock Entrance

56

57

Victoria Wharf

Limehouse Cut Entrance   Hough's Wharf

Dover Wharf   Kidney Stairs

Blyth's Wharf · Stepney Boro' Council · Limehouse Gener

58   59   60   61

North Bank
LimekiIn Dock to Union Docks Wharf

Limekiln Dock   Dundee Wharf

Limehouse Pier   Limehouse Hole Stairs

Buchanan's Wharf

66* (36)   67* (37)   68* (38)

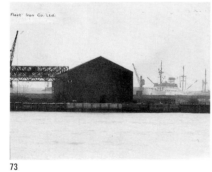

Fleet Iron Co. Ltd.

Union Docks Wharf

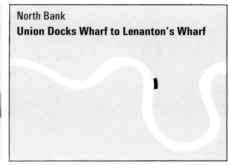

North Bank
Union Docks Wharf to Lenanton's Wharf

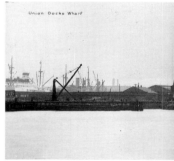

Union Docks Wharf

73   74   75

Son, Ltd.

North Bank
**Lenanton's Wharf to
Atlas Chemical Works**

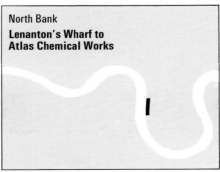

John Lenanton & Son Ltd.   Torrington Arms Stairs   Oak Wharf

London Wharf

80   81* (42)   82* (43)

111

63* (34) 64* (35) 65

70 71 72

77* (41) 78 79

84* (45) 85 86

Glengall Wharf

Glengall Causeway · Atlas Chemical Works

87

88

North Bank
Atlas Chemical Works to Le Bas Wharf

Atlas Chemical Works

89

Snowdon's Wharf

Winkley's Wharf

Le Bas Wharf

EDWARD LE BAS

94

95

96

97

Wharf · Rose's Wharf

St. Andrew's Wharf

Cocoanut Stairs · Guelph Wharf

101

102

103

104

North Bank
Burrell's Wharf to St David's Wharf

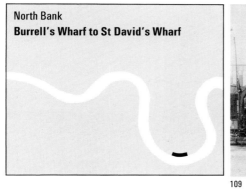

Burrell's Wharf

Maconochie's Wharf

109

110

111

othy's Wharf · Mellich's Wharf · Fenner's Wharf · Millwall Dock Entrance Lock · Workmen's Dwellings

91 92* (46) 93* (47)

Bank
s Wharf to Burrell's Wharf

Le Bas Wharf

Providence Iron Works

Ferguson's

98 99 100

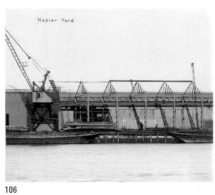

Napier Yard

Venesta Wharf

Burrell's Wharf

106 107* (48) 108* (49)

Nelson Wharf · Shaws Wharf · BRIDGE BUILDERS

MATT. T. SHAW & C?? CONSTRUCTIONAL ENGINEERS MILLWALL

Locke's Wharf

113 114 115

St. David's
Wharf

116

North Bank
St David's Wharf to Island Gardens

St. David's Wharf   Owen Parry's Wharf

117* (50)

Felstead

118* (51)

Wharf

119* (52)

Millwall Boiler Works   Livingston Wharf

JOHN FRASER & SON

120* (53)

Midland Oil Wharf

CLARKS' ANTI-FOULING COMPOSITIONS FOR SHIPS' BOTTOMS

121

Johnson's
Draw Dock

H. CLARK & SONS Ltd

122

Calder's Wharf

123* (54)

Greenwich
Footway
Tunnel   Island Gardens

124* (55)

The Complete Riverscape Panorama

Deptford Power Station, with its smoking chimneys, dominates this 1930s aerial photograph. A steam collier can be seen discharging at the power station's jetty and, just behind, the General Steam Navigation Company's paddle steamer, *Golden Eagle*, lies moored at Deptford Creek Tier. A cargo ship lies further down river, at Greenwich Tier, discharging her cargo into lighters.

In the foreground are new blocks of council houses and demolition of nineteenth-century terraces is taking place. Across the river is the southern tip of the Isle of Dogs, stretching from Maconachie's Wharf, on the left, to Island Gardens.

South Bank
Royal Naval College to Dodd's Wharf

Facsimile reproduction
with original annotation.
Each titled block represents a
single dissected folded section.

*Selected Riverscapes (page number)

Royal Naval College

1* (58)

Greenwich Observatory   Greenwich Pier

2* (59)

Ship Tavern   Garden Stairs

3* (60)

7

Electric Welding Works

8

9

Talbot's Wharf   Victoria & Norway Wharf

10

Deptford Creek

15* (62)

General Steam Navigation Co Ltd
The Stowage

16* (63)

South Bank
**The Stowage to
Deptford Supply Reserve Depôt**

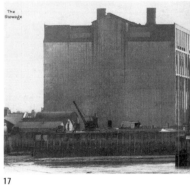

The Stowage

17

22

Borthwick's Cold Store

THOMAS BORTHWICK AND SONS LTD

23

Payne's Paper Wharf

PAYNES PAPER WHARF

24* (64)

Watergate Stairs

25* (65)

Dodd's Wharf

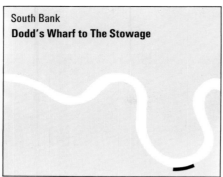

South Bank
Dodd's Wharf to The Stowage

Dodd's Wharf

Billingsgate Dock

5

6

Dreadnought Yard – Tilbury Contracting & Dredging Cº Ltd

Phoenix Wharf – S.M Gas Cº

12

13

14

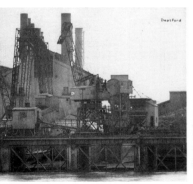

Deptford Power Station

Lower Watergate

19

20

21

Palmer's Cold Stores

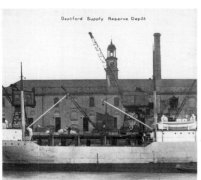

Deptford Supply Reserve Depot

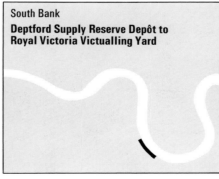

South Bank
Deptford Supply Reserve Depôt to
Royal Victoria Victualling Yard

Deptford Supply Reserve Depôt

27

28

Deptford Supply Reserve Depôt

Royal Victoria Victualling Yard

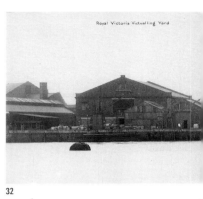

29* (66)　　　30* (67)　　　31　　　32

Royal Victoria Victualling Yard

South Bank
Royal Victoria Victualling Yard to Greenland Entrance Lock

37* (69)　　　38　　　39

Deptford Wharf
Deadman's Dock

St. George's Stairs

St. George's Wharf

Southl

44　　　45　　　46　　　47

Greenland Entrance Lock

Greenland Sheds
(P.L.A.)

Stairs

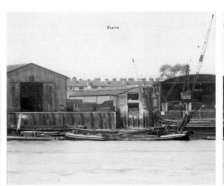

Redriff Wharf

Odessa Wharf

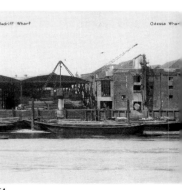

51　　　52　　　53　　　54

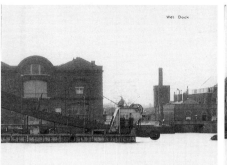

Wet Dock

Royal Victoria

Royal Victoria Victualling Yard

34

35

36* (68)

Royal Victoria Victualling Yard

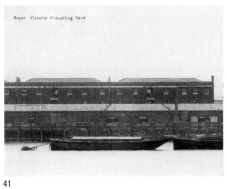

Wet Dock

41

42

43

Dog & Duck P.H.   Dog & Duck Stairs

Greenland Entrance Lock

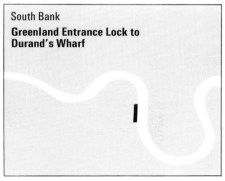

South Bank

Greenland Entrance Lock to Durand's Wharf

49

50

"Condemned Hole"   Commercial Wharf   Commercial Dock Pier

Barnard's Wharf

South Wharf

56

57

58* (70)

South Bank
Durand's Wharf to Upper Ordnance Wh

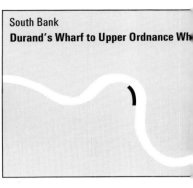

59* (71)

60* (72)

61* (73)

66* (74)

67* (75)

68

69

73

74

75

76

80

81

82

83* (76)

84* (77)

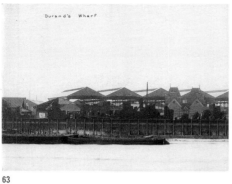

Durand's Wharf

Lawrence's Wharf

Somerset Wharf   Albion Wharf   Danzic Wharf

63

64

65

Upper Ordnance Wharf

South Bank
Upper Ordnance Wharf to Upper Globe Wharf

Upper Ordnance Wharf

Pageant Wharf

L.C.C. Fire Station   Pageant Wharf

Lavender Pumping Station (P.L.A.)

W.B. DICK & CO.

71

72

Crown Lead Works

Globe Stairs   Upper Globe Wharf

South Bank
Upper Globe Wharf to Dinorwic Wharf

78

79

Surrey Commercial Wharf   Dinorwic Wharf

South Bank
Dinorwic Wharf to Thames Tunnel Mills

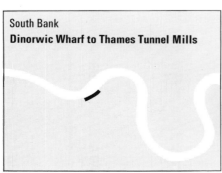

Dinorwic Wharf

Surrey Entrance Lock

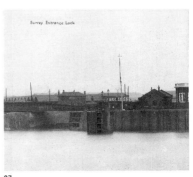

86

87

88

89

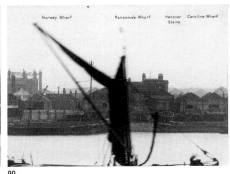

90

91

96* (78)

97* (79)

98* (80)

99* (81)

104* (84)

105* (85)

106* (86)

107* (87)

111* (90)

112* (91)

113* (92)

114* (93)

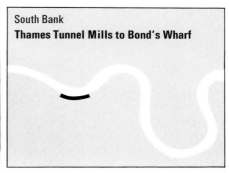

South Bank
Thames Tunnel Mills to Bond's Wharf

93 94 95

101* (83) 102 103

Bank
's Wharf to Tower Bridge

108* (88) 109* (89) 110

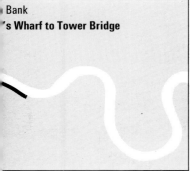

116* (94) 117* (95) 117A* (95)

South Bank
Tower Bridge to London Bridge

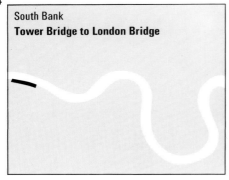

Tower Bridge Wharf

Mark Brown's Wharves   Pickle Herring

118* (96)   119* (97)   119A   120* (98)

Wharf   St. Olave's Wharf   Pickle Herring Stairs

Stanton's Wharf   Symon's Wharf

Gun & Shot   Griffin's Wharves   South Thames Wharf   Battlebridge Stairs   Griffin's Wharf

William's Wharves

121* (99)   122   122A   123   124

Hay's Wharf

Hay's Dock   Humphery's Wharf

Cotton's Wharf

125* (100)   126* (101)   127   128* (102)

Chamberlain's Wharf   Offices

Topping's Wharf   Sun Wharf   Fenning's Wharf

129* (103)   130   130A